The Sleepwalker's Dream

A Novel

Dhrubajyoti Borah

SPEAKING
TIGER

SPEAKING TIGER PUBLISHING PVT. LTD
4381/4, Ansari Road, Daryaganj
New Delhi 110002

First published in paperback by Speaking Tiger 2016

ISBN: 978-93-86050-04-5
eISBN: 978-93-86050-02-1

10 9 8 7 6 5 4 3 2 1

Typeset in Adobe Garamond Pro by SÜRYA, New Delhi
Printed at Sanat Printers, Kundli

Dr Dhrubajyoti Borah, a medical doctor by profession, is a Guwahati-based Assamese writer and novelist. In a literary career spanning over three decades he has published many critically acclaimed works of fiction and non-fiction, including novels, monographs on history, travelogues and collections of articles. He received the Sahitya Akademi Award in 2009. This is his first novel in English.

1

THE FALLEN AUTUMN leaves crunched softly underfoot, a crackly sound interspersed with heavy breathing. The surrounding forest was a web of silence.

The sky above was a pale shade of blue already heavy with the cold of the approaching winter.

Pale, cold and silent, the snow-capped mountains and the grey-green forests on the foothills appeared to be quite near. The stony ridges on the slopes, even the jutting rocks and crevices between them, the grey-white snowline, everything appeared crystal clear in the rarefied mountain air.

A small band of people trudged slowly, trying to find the way down the steep mountainside.

June's breathing was fast and shallow. It was painful for her to inhale the cold mountain air. She could hear her own breathing and through it the throbbing of her beating heart. She was trailing the band by a good thirty paces, her right shoulder numb from the weight of the gun she carried and her mind strangely vacant, emptied of all thoughts.

She felt as if she was walking in a present that was already past and each breath she took felt like a breath taken in some distant past.

They were approaching a small clearing, a narrow slanting meadow covered with grass and strewn with rocks of different sizes. Jagged outcroppings of rocks that rose like small mounds were scattered on it. The group, which was travelling under the thin conifer forests of the mountain slope, stopped silently before entering the open patch.

It was already late afternoon and the band had been walking since early morning, lugging their baggage, equipment and the makeshift stretcher. Their injured leader continued to waft between consciousness and unconsciousness as he lay on it, with spells of guttural groans interspersed with a stream of unspeakable obscenities.

The four persons in charge of transporting the stretcher carried it on their shoulders in pairs at a time—the other two then carried the guns, bags and blankets.

It wasn't easy to carry the unconscious person on a stretcher over the steep and tortuous mountain track. The band had been doing exactly that for the last three days, frequently changing shoulders and exchanging duties. Occasionally, the boys would put the blankets over their injured leader's legs, removing them hurriedly the moment he stirred.

The person now leading the group went cautiously to the edge of the clearing while the others waited silently. His name was Ron. He surveyed his surroundings, trying to get a general feel of the area. He then looked up at the sky, scrutinizing it in a thoughtful manner and moving his head from side to side as if he was trying to hear a particular sound.

Yesterday, when they were crossing a similar meadow, a helicopter had suddenly appeared over the shoulder of the mountain and fired at them.

The memory rankled. It was so vivid yet so unreal....

Ron cautiously went forward, crossed the meadow swiftly and looked down beyond what looked like a slope. He descended a little, disappearing from their view. After some time he reappeared, climbed up and rapidly crossed the meadows. As soon as he entered the tree-covered area, the distant drone of a helicopter became audible.

Inside the clump of trees, everybody instinctively hunched their shoulders, as if trying to draw their necks into their chests like tortoises, and scanned the sky with anxious eyes. Some hunkered down immediately.

The two stretcher-bearers squatted with the stretcher still on their shoulders. Soon, a small speck of a helicopter appeared in the sky and then disappeared rapidly.

'We'll stay here tonight,' said Ron.

The two stretcher-bearers placed the stretcher down on four tripods made of split bamboo so that it did not touch the ground.

Everybody put down their packs and stretched their limbs in relief.

The leader on the stretcher remained unconscious.

～

It was early afternoon that day, when the first shell had exploded inside the camp.

The sun was very bright that day, the sky cloudless,

and the whole camp had shimmered like a mirage in the bright sunshine.

There was an eerie high-pitched whine in the air for a second or two, followed by a deafening sound and a crashing jolt that shook the ground as in an earthquake.

Silence followed for a few moments, after which a tall plume of dirty white smoke rose to the sky. June, sitting in front of her hut in another part of the sprawling camp, felt as if a strong gust of wind had hit her. She saw Ron leaping out of a hut followed by two or three boys.

'They are shelling us!' he had screamed.

People ran out of the huts like excited red ants.

Then a second shell burst in yet another part of the camp. 'They are attacking us!' somebody had shouted hoarsely near her. All she saw was a contorted face, but she couldn't make out who it was. She instinctively started running towards Ron in the distance.

The air was filled with shrill whining and mortar shells burst like firecrackers near the outer defences below.

They had subconsciously expected the attack, but had lived in a state of denial, refusing to believe in the inevitable.

They had built the large armed camp in an outlying part of a foreign country—Bhutan. The area was quite inaccessible and sparsely populated. And from the sanctuary of that armed camp they had carried out their political and militant activity against their own country—India. It is true that such insurgent camps had come to abound in the upper reaches of Myanmar where various tribal ethnic groups hid in their lairs.

They had spent more than three years in that camp! Yes, more than three years! They knew the local government didn't look at them kindly. June had heard the top leaders in the camp talking about trying a diplomatic engagement with the government of the country and planning alternatives, but no action took place and, amidst the increased uncertainty, the attack suddenly occurred.

By the time she had reached Ron, June could see that he was already ordering everyone to gather as much arms, ammunition, implements and supplies as they could and assemble near the eastern part of the camp. The attack was from the west.

'Stay close to me,' Ron ordered her.

June gasped at the devastation before her eyes. All the main wooden buildings of the camp were already flattened or blown to smithereens. The meeting hall, council chamber, the offices were all gone. Some were burning fiercely. People were running helter-skelter carrying various items towards the eastern slopes.

We may have to leave camp and move to the forests and the mountains, June thought with a shiver, and ran towards the arms store behind Ron.

At that moment, mortar shells started bursting inside the camp.

'They are closing in!' she heard Ron shouting. 'Get your arms, move…faster, faster…'

It was in this way that they had been blasted out of their fortified mountain camp, without putting up any real resistance.

2

JUNE LEANED ON a tree trunk when the helicopter appeared and closed her eyes.

She remained leaning, with her backpack on her shoulders, the gun in one hand and a plastic jerrycan of water in the other.

Ron, the leader of the band, came towards her briskly.

'Are you all right?' The concern in his voice sounded very genuine. He took the jerrycan and the gun from her and said in a soft voice, 'Keep your spirits up. Once we cross the next mountain, the descent will be easy.'

June nodded. She could not really understand what Ron was saying. She took a step forward.

'You seem to be limping,' Ron said. 'Have you injured your legs somewhere?'

'It's only cramps.' She hastily added, 'Cramps from walking on this steep path, up and down.'

'You must rest today, completely. You don't have to do anything today. Just rest and massage your legs. If only I could heat a stone to put over the cramped muscles, it would help.'

She followed him silently, touched by his concern. She tried not to limp.

They reached the others who were sitting under the trees. Ron picked up a stone, and said, 'This should do. I will heat this stone for you. It should take care of your cramps.'

'We will have to heat some more stones to put under the blankets,' one of the group said, pointing to the unconscious leader. He was one of the stretcher-bearers. 'It was too cold last night, as was the night before. He won't survive another night like that.'

Ron nodded. Last night had been freezing.

They had six blankets between the nine members of the group. At least two were required for the injured leader and one for June. The remaining three blankets would have to be shared by seven people. Ron reviewed the situation again mentally. *Yes, three blankets for seven people.* Although he had a worn shawl inside his backpack and all of them wore sweaters and cotton quilted jackets, those were really no protection against the biting mountain cold. *Today I will have to take measures to help us withstand the cold*, he thought.

'We have come quite a long way today,' Sona, the stretcher-bearer, said. Ron nodded. Yes, they had been able to come quite far, leaving the danger zone far behind.

'It may be little safer here.'

'Relatively,' Ron agreed. 'We will have to do something. We will have to build some kind of shelter, even if it's only for one night.'

Everybody silently nodded.

So they cut down some long leafy branches from the

trees around, taking care to make as little sound as they could. Then they pushed the branches into the ground in two parallel rows. The fronds were bent together from both sides and lashed. A long jagged structure soon took shape. They then put plastic sheets over it and covered it with more leafy branches and dry leaves.

Within two or three hours, a long hut-like structure was ready.

June suddenly remembered a long-forgotten lesson from her social studies school textbooks, about how primitive man built shelters against the elements. *We have now become primitive people*, she thought, quite amused by the thought of them following primitive practices.

With sundown nearing, it was already beginning to get cold. A bitingly cold wind began to rise, obstructing the already waning warmth from the setting sun. As the cold increased in large regular surges, the leaf hut seemed too fragile and inadequate to resist it.

We are in for a freezing time, June thought, *yes, really as cold as ice.*

They then hurriedly put the stretcher with the leader on it inside the hut and built a small fire at one end. Ron placed a circle of fist-sized stones around the base of the fire, like a garland, to heat up. He gestured towards June, pointing at a stone in the fire, 'That's for you.'

The fire was lit during daytime so that the glow would not betray their presence. They were also adept at making smokeless fires.

'We need to keep the fire going throughout the night,' Ron said 'I hope it will at least keep the chill out of the hut.'

'The light and smoke won't show outside, sir,' quipped one of the boys who was tending the fire. 'The sides of the house are layered with black plastic. I have put lots of green branches in the hole above, which will filter and distribute whatever little smoke there is. The trees above will take care of the rest. We need to gather as many pine needles and dry twigs as we can.'

June looked thoughtfully at the boy.

He was busy tending the fire. In its light, his face glowed faintly, making his eyebrows and cheeks prominent.

He looks like an ape, June thought. Then she chided herself for thinking like that. She was sitting at the other side of the fire near the foot of the stretcher.

The late afternoon meal consisted of a little rice and lentils cooked together into a gruel in the large battered pot, the only one they had with them. Ron had started to carefully ration out the food from the second day of their journey. On the first day, they had no time or opportunity to eat except at night and even then, it had been a cold meal of moistened parched rice with some salt sprinkled in it. They had managed to carry only a little food when they escaped.

Rice, dal and salt—at least they had a warm meal today. June tried not to think about food.

At night she could hear the soft breathing of the stretcher-bearers from the other end of the hut. She was lying wide awake near the stretcher, the fire near her head lending her a faint warmth. The leader in the stretcher had been still and silent for a very long time. She tried to catch the sound of his breathing but couldn't. She suddenly felt afraid—*has something happened to him? Is he unconscious or in a deep sleep? Or has he…?* She felt a shiver run down her spine and shuddered inadvertently.

The inside of the hut was becoming uncomfortable, the cold air mixed with smoke making it oppressive. She felt suffocated.

Ron and the other companions were nowhere to be seen. *Where have they gone?* she asked herself anxiously. *At this hour, in the dead of night? Could they possibly have gone somewhere?*

She raised herself on her elbows. A little further away, a plastic sheet had been placed on a bed of pine needles. There was a blanket atop it but there was no sign that anybody had slept there. Beyond the opening of the hut, through the trunks of the trees of the small forest, she could see the sky bright with moonlight. *It must be a full moon night*, she thought. She tried to remember the days of the lunar month but soon lost track and gave up. She had prided herself on being able to remember the English date and the day of the lunar month simultaneously. Now she could not. Even her memory was playing tricks on her.

3

Outside, the forest was bathed in brilliant moonlight.

It was so bright that June was amazed. Then she began to feel apprehensive. The whole mountainside, the gaps through the outline of the peaks in the distance, the rock-strewn meadows were aglow with an eerie blueish light.

The moonlight in the mountains is different, June thought. It was cold and frightening, not like the warm golden, comforting glow of the moonlight of her village or the little hilly town where she grew up. Can moonlight be so different, or was it her memory playing tricks on her?

When she had come out of the cocoon of her blanket to go outside, she never thought she would see such sinister moonlight. Before stepping out of the low leafy hut, she looked at the figure on the stretcher with trepidation and for a moment thought the stretcher was empty. Then, slowly, she could make out the outline of the figure lying under the blankets. It was dark and smoky from the embers of the fire inside the hut. She had thought that her senses were leaving her in that cold, strange darkness.

She shivered violently once she was out in the open. She darted in, picked up her blanket and wrapped herself with it.

Ron and the other members of the group were nowhere to be seen.

She became even more frightened.

On such full moon nights in her village, jackals would howl in the distance, in the open paddy fields, beyond the bamboo thickets. She used to be afraid of the howling when she was a little girl, but when she came home from the hill town where she studied, the same chorus felt so reassuring, as if the jackals were welcoming her back to the village.

She wished they would howl now, pointing their muzzles towards the moon. She strained her ears to pick up any sound, but the entire mountainside was silent, totally silent in the ghostly glow of the moon.

Though she was afraid of the shadows of the night, she went ahead through the ghostly shadows cast by the tall conifers towards the open meadow.

A shadow detached itself from the dark trees the moment she stepped into the moonlight.

'What are you doing here?'

June gave a start at the low harsh voice.

'I cannot sleep.'

'You shouldn't come out like that. You'll catch a cold.'

'I have this on,' she unwrapped the blanket and held out the two ends in her hands like wings. The heavy blanket flapped slowly like a wet flag in the cold mountain air.

'Wrap yourself up quickly,' said the boy. 'At least you had the good sense to bring that out.'

'Are you on sentry duty?'

'Till midnight, then I'll go to sleep. One of the louts

now sleeping inside the hut will relieve me. They must be snoring. Are they?'

'Not yet.'

'Go back to the hut, double quick.'

'Oh, it's cold and stuffy there and I can't sleep. I don't know where sleep has fled. I was so tired in the afternoon.... where is Ron sir?'

'They have gone there,' the sentry pointed with the muzzle of his gun towards the open meadow. 'Said he wants to see the terrain ahead in the moonlight.'

June shivered and waited, hoping that the sentry would not ask her to go back again.

'You should go back in' he said in a soft tone. 'Sir may get angry.'

'I don't want to. I am not going,' she said bluntly. 'I am afraid to stay there all alone—I mean, all of them are sleeping. It is so silent. And our leader is not moving at all. I did not even hear him breathing. There is no sound at all.... I'd rather stay here.'

'Let us at least move into the shadows' the sentry said. Then he added as an afterthought, a little reluctantly, 'I am also worried about him, his condition does not seem good to me.'

'Oh, don't say that,' a shiver crept into her voice.

Their breath came out in puffs of condensed vapour.

'We have been carrying him for the last three days. He is floating between consciousness and unconsciousness. And when he becomes conscious, he is not able to speak coherently. That is because he is not awake for long. If he is conscious for a longer time, his speech will also improve. Last night, I think, he recognized me. Yes, I have the distinct feeling that he recognized me. But today he was asleep for the whole day. Even now he is in deep sleep… or is he unconscious?'

They fell silent.

Neither of them wanted to talk about the leader or the situation they were in. Without speaking, they sat down on the ground near each other with their backs on the trunk of a large conifer.

Suddenly, June had that familiar feeling of unreality—as if the events of the last three days were not real. She realized that it was not a dream. *How can it be a dream? I am fully awake and shivering in this monstrous cold!* June told herself.

Both of them looked towards the rock-strewn meadow in front of them.

The meadow appeared blueish, ghostly, yet infinitely more beautiful! Soon, shadows started floating over it, light, airy, dancing shadows. Possibly, some woolly clouds had drifted below the moon. But she was too afraid to look up and did not want to know about the cause of the fleeting dancing shadows.

4

THEY TALKED SOFTLY as if they were under a spell.

The wind had become stronger, whistling softly among the leaves of the trees above. When a strong gust blew, the soft whine became a wail.

'You know, I am always a little afraid of this cry of the pines,' June said.

'It's nothing but the wind.'

'I know, but still, sometimes it really sounds like a girl wailing.'

'I have never thought about it like that. To me the sound is more like the howling of foxes.'

'No, no, foxes don't howl like that. We have a big pack of them in my village. I think there are no foxes or jackals here in the mountains. I wish there were.'

'I don't know. I have been told that there are Himalayan wolves around here. They are big and fierce creatures.'

'Oh, I really dislike those fierce pack hunters.'

'And leopards too. They say many leopards prowl in these areas, even the rare snow leopards. One may just choose to make a visit here. This must be the time to prowl.'

'Don't scare me.' June cast furtive glances into the ink-blue darkness around her. 'I wouldn't like to meet one of them here,' she said.

Trying to keep up the conversation, June said, 'Have you noticed how cruel the eyes of the leopard are? I first noticed it in the zoo. And from then I have always recalled the cold, cruel look of the leopard with fear.'

'It surely is a stealthy creature,' the boy said. 'And cunning too.'

They continued their conversation like this in fits and starts, jumping from topic to topic but never mentioning the condition of the leader again, or the plight they were in.

'It's getting late,' the boy said. 'Don't you think you should go in? The cold is also increasing.'

'I will wait until Ron and the other boys return.'

'He may be angry. May even scold me for letting you stay here like this.'

'Let him. I don't care,' she said defiantly.

The boy just shrugged his shoulder in the darkness.

The meadow suddenly became dark. It was as if the bright moonlight had been sucked in by the ground, by the mountains! The outlines of the stone outcroppings of the meadow had vanished.

'What is happening?' June sounded worried. 'They have not returned yet. And it's so dark.'

'Only clouds; it should clear again.'

They remained silent for some time. With the disappearance of the meadow into the darkness, the surroundings seemed unearthly.

'Did you hear that?' June suddenly said.

'What? What?'

'That sound—like howling?'

They both could hear it now though it was faint. A long throaty howl resounded somewhere in the distance. After a few such calls, other voices joined in, and each sound seemed to come from different places,

'Wolves! Those are wolves calling.'

'My God!' June's voice trembled. 'What should we do now?'

'Nothing. They are very far off. The first one to call was the male leader of the pack. Then the other members responded. The wind has carried those sounds to this side.'

'I am worried they may attack us. I told you I didn't like pack hunters. There is something very cruel and merciless about pack hunting, cruel and cowardly too.'

'That's your opinion. But have you ever thought about us? Aren't we also like pack hunters?'

The darkness started to lift then. The clouds that covered the moon had possibly moved away. The meadow again shone brilliantly. The ghostly, blueish moonlight returned and it was then that they heard snatches of talk floating in from the meadow. Ron and the boys were returning.

They stood up hurriedly.

Soon they could make out the outlines of three people returning through the meadow.

The sentry stood at full attention, his gun in position. And June tried to melt into the darkness.

'What you two are doing here?' Ron's voice was sharp.

'I couldn't sleep. So I came out looking for you.'

'How is our leader?' He sounded reproachful.

'He is in deep sleep. Never called out and didn't move either.'

'Oh,' said Ron. Then he quickly added. 'Look at the breath coming out of your mouths like steam from a pressure cooker. Ha ha.' He laughed a little nervously and then fanned the vapours coming out of his own mouth with his palms. 'Let's go in. You will freeze to death here. I think your sentry duty is also nearly over, isn't it?' Ron tried to peer into his watch.

Just as they were about to enter the hut, a loud grunting sound came from the stretcher.

They all rushed forward.

Everything appeared like a blur to June.

Everybody crowded around the stretcher. The stretcher-bearers who had slept at the foot of the stretcher got up, looking worried, and with their sleep-swollen eyes goggled at the leader. Someone lit up the nearly dead fire with utter disregard for the safety norms they followed. Smoke and a slightly acrid smell of burning leaves and pine needles filled the small hut. Shadows danced on the inner wall of the hut, making it appear like a primitive stone cave or, June thought in disgust, *like the insides of the bowels of a slithering serpent*.

The leader's eyes were open, burning bright like a leopard's.

Only his eyes could be seen, more defiant and questioning than cruel.

Everything felt so unreal, so out of place. She wanted to melt into the surrounding darkness at the back of the hut.

And then she heard, as if floating in from a great distance, the words of their leader, 'Where are we? How have I come here?'

5

THE VERY NEXT day, after the leader gained consciousness, June realized that something dreadful had happened.

That day, June could make out that the leader was not moving his legs at all. And he was moving his arms only very feebly. She could also make out that he was not yet aware of it.

She dreaded the moment when he would realize that he was paralysed from the waist down. How would he take it? A man whom she knew to be a highly confident, arrogant and intimidating person even when he talked in a friendly way.

Her heart beat faster at the mere thought of it.

How would he take it? Would she have to tell him anything? Would she have to break the news to him? What should she tell him? And how? She played different versions of what she would have to tell him in her mind and rejected every one of them.

She really dreaded the moment.

The journey so far had been a nightmare.

It seemed so unreal as if she was traversing the mountains in a bad, opaque dream!

Her body didn't feel as her own. The limbs felt leaden, heavy and plastic-like, loaded with extra weight.

She knew that she had long ago, nearly at the beginning, stopped thinking or worrying. She responded to any situation passively and mechanically. She had left all thinking and worrying to Ron and had become indifferent to whatever happened.

When Ron put her in charge of looking after the leader, she had accepted the responsibility without thinking about it.

'The stretcher-bearers will only carry our leader,' Ron had told her. 'You will be totally in charge of looking after him, feeding him, cleaning him, keeping him company, everything. Do you understand?'

That was before the leader had gained consciousness.

And when he did, a small intense area of concern quickened within her numbed, indifferent brain. She became angry with herself for this concern and then she was surprised at her own anger.

When the group broke their journey under a shady knoll and all the boys sat thankfully on the ground, she went to the leader and asked him, 'Are you feeling better today, sir?'

He looked at her in a strange way, as if trying to place her, recognize her. He then smiled wanly and nodded his head, but June had the feeling that he had not recognized her.

At the same time, she became a little frightened by his smile, signifying gloom rather than friendliness.

'I feel very weak,' he suddenly said in a loud clear voice. 'I am barely able to move my hands. See how slowly they move.'

June's heart fluttered. She looked at the movement of the hands he was showing her with a sense of mounting dread. But he did not speak about his legs.

'I feel sleepy all the time,' he said again. 'I don't know whether it is good or bad. It can make you weaker, you know.'

She was at a loss for words. Then she stammered, 'I think sleeping is good for you.'

'You think so?' he asked. Then with a faint smile he turned on his side and went back to sleep.

June saw Ron watching her. He inclined his head and asked if everything was all right. She nodded her head in answer and moved away.

She went and sat with the other boys who were sitting together at a distance, talking amongst themselves in low tones. Nearly everybody had to carry the stretcher at one point or the other during their journey, except Ron and June. In the beginning Ron tried to carry the stretcher and did a stint or two, but the others refused to let him carry it again. Pradip, one of the boys, argued that Ron was needed to lead from the front, to find the way, so should not distract himself by carrying the stretcher. Ron tried to protest, but Pradip, Kumbang and the other boys were insistent and Ron had to ultimately accept their view. He tried to distribute the work amongst the others in a fair manner.

When June plopped down on the ground, she could sense that the boys had abruptly stopped their conversation, perhaps because they did not want her to hear what they were saying.

So she started to talk herself, 'Though the leader has now gained full consciousness, he is still very weak. He drifts off to sleep quite often. I think sleep will only help him, don't you think so? Your effort in carrying him against such odds has really paid off.'

The ice was broken and the boys became voluble.

On the first three days, when the leader was unconscious, the boys carrying him had talked freely. The stretcher-bearers complained about the weight, about their sore shoulders and openly said how fast they could have moved if they did not have to carry the leader. But they only spoke aloud when they were out of Ron's earshot.

Now that the leader had regained consciousness, they recollected the difficulties of the time and joked about them.

'How difficult it was to carry him over the uneven mountain track!' said Kumbang, who was given to making jokes even in the worst of situations. 'Many a time, while I was carrying him, I thought I would trip and fall, and then the leader would fall too. Bringing it to an end at last!'

Everybody smiled, but nobody laughed.

Then Ron joined them and June immediately shrank a little in his presence—she always did. Though she liked Ron very much, his presence always made her self-conscious.

Then Pradip said, 'It will possibly be better if we can

fashion a chair-like contraption. Then it may be much easier to carry him over this path. It is not very tough to carry the stretcher up, but going down, especially on craggy uneven paths is really very difficult.'

'Yes, a chair may be much easier to carry.'

'It might really help,' added someone else.

June noticed that Ron was silently looking from one speaker to the other. He was possibly evaluating the idea of a chair in his mind.

'We cannot do that,' June suddenly interjected.

'Why?' Everybody looked at her in surprise.

They were startled by her urgent tone. They had not heard her voice much during the journey.

She fumbled for words. Words were refusing to form inside her brain. She raised her eyes and looked at Ron. She could see that his intense gaze was encouraging so she blurted out, 'I think his legs are paralysed. He cannot move them at all. He is not yet aware of it, but I think it is paralysis.'

She looked at Ron and the boys, while they looked back at her intently. She continued, nearly breathless, 'If we carry him in a chair, it might harm him greatly.'

Everybody sat silently for a long time.

6

'FOR FOUR NIGHTS they carried me on this ramshackle stretcher!' the leader mumbled. He had taken to mumbling to himself, his words sometimes distinct, sometimes unclear. The stretcher-bearers could hear him sometimes—and June, who was asked by Ron to walk near the stretcher, could also hear him.

She responded at first but soon realized that the leader didn't answer her but kept on talking to himself. Then she stopped replying but tried to catch his words instead.

'Four nights! Imagine!' the leader droned. 'And I am quite heavy—it is truly remarkable that they managed to bring me out with them this far. They say they had to literally shoot their way out at one place, avoided a near ambush at another! Remarkable, truly remarkable. It shows true grit…'

June shuddered at the thought of the encounter, which was really a near thing, but she was not even aware of the ambush because Ron had suddenly taken them into a detour.

'Ah, think of it, think of it! Yes, they were really handicapped by me on the stretcher during all these days!'

His mumble became indistinct. He stopped for some time, then restarted. 'Why, I don't have any memory of the encounter or of that near escape. They say I keep drifting in and out of sleep and they probably are right. It cannot be untrue just because I do not have any memory of what happened. Yes, it can't be untrue.'

'Where is the girl?' the leader called out loudly.

'Sir? Are you calling anyone?' the head-end stretcher-bearer asked.

'Yes, the girl. June, where is she?'

The stretcher-bearer called out for June.

She came immediately and asked, 'Do you need anything, sir?'

'Where is Ron?'

'He has gone ahead to find the right direction,' she replied.

'I must tell you one thing. You shouldn't have done it.'

'What, sir?' June's voice became anxious.

'You shouldn't have wasted a whole day and a night like that. When I came to my senses, you wasted the whole day.'

'It was only a day, sir,' June said. 'We would have camped for the night anyway. We waited for you to recover a little. And you did.'

'No, you wasted a lot of valuable time, don't I know? We could have continued like this. You think you have travelled far away from the danger zone? You think you are safe now? I don't think so.'

June and the stretcher-bearers exchanged anxious glances. The leader continued.

'You don't have any idea that the enemy can surround you in concentric circles. You already had an encounter and a near ambush. That can happen again. They can lie in wait for you in different places, different times. The paths leading down from the mountains are all known. You have to follow those paths. You can't deviate much. Do you realize that or you don't?'

'Yes, sir.'

'What, "yes, sir?" You don't seem to understand.'

June and the stretcher-bearers felt relieved when Ron came back and ordered a short rest break. The group sat under some trees, while Ron and June sat near the stretcher. The leader went on speaking to June but she knew his words were mainly directed at Ron.

'I told you, you can't deviate much from the known mountain tracks. These are not plains. At places there are unclimbable mountain faces, steep without any toehold. There are deep chasms, giddy drops which you can't negotiate. There are deep valleys with thick forests, marshy land, even swamps that you can't cross and unfordable mountain streams. That leaves you only with certain areas, some pathways by which you can go down, where you can cross the mountain ridges. The enemy also knows this. They know that it's not very difficult to keep a watch on the tracks you will have to follow at one time or the other.'

June looked at Ron, a little perplexed. Ron gave her a faint smile, then said to the leader, 'I am trying to take all the precautions I can, sir. Now that you are all right, I feel so relieved. Nobody knows these areas better than you do.'

June saw the leader's face light up and a satisfied smile spread on his face. June felt happy and relieved at the same time as she remembered hearing in the camp that the leader knew the mountains like the back of his hands.

The leader ate the two biscuits and the water June gave him. He looked content and began mumbling again. June tried to make out what he was saying.

'And one whole day and night they waited and wasted for me. They wanted to make sure that I would fully regain my senses, that I was comfortable! I had voided my guts and bladder after I became conscious. Oh, the shame of it. It's still burning my face. I had no control over those acts, but they were so caring, so considerate. They acted as if it was the most normal thing that could have happened! Ron even told me that it was very good that it had happened, otherwise my health would have been affected, He was secretly worried that I had not passed urine or stool for nearly three days…'

After some time, June and the stretcher-bearers stopped trying to hear what the leader was saying as the going was rough and it was a big strain trying to do so. And anyway they couldn't always make out what he was saying.

But the leader kept mumbling…

He is only thinking aloud, June thought.

And the leader was actually doing that, mumbling thoughts to himself. His thoughts were not always coherent, but jumped from one subject to the other. Sometimes he himself was not fully aware about what he was thinking. But at other times his thoughts were very clear.

'And that wisp of a girl? What's her name?' the leader said. 'Ah June, June! What a strange name that is. She had silently taken over my nursing. She had insisted I should have a sponge bath and with warm water, she rubbed me all over, never hesitating, never faltering for a moment. She said she had no nurse's training, but she took to nursing as if it was the most natural thing in the world...I can feel her presence near me always. Though I had come to my senses, I was still groggy. Often, I couldn't make any sense of what was happening around me. I have a feeling, a very distinct feeling, that the world has become a very strange place, a very dreadful place...'

7

'The first feeling that I had after gaining consciousness was one of great fright, you know....'

The leader was talking to Ron. Once he had gained consciousness and could talk, there was no holding him back.

'I realized that I couldn't move my legs, they wouldn't move at all. It's not that I didn't try, but I felt my body did not exist below my waist. A sudden flash of pain would shoot down and only then would I become aware of my lower body.'

'You must not get excited,' Ron told him and he looked up to June as if he sought support from her. 'It's all a passing phase, a temporary result of your injury.'

'But I know I am paralysed—paralysed below my navel. I have no feeling in my thighs, in my groin, nowhere.'

'You were nearly unconscious for much of the time, drifting between sleep and wakefulness.'

'Wait, I feel I was conscious at times, possibly for stretches, as you said. For I distinctly remember that I could hear the boys speak, could understand what they were saying. And soon I became aware that I was being carried somewhere. I have no memory of going to sleep, of unconsciousness.'

'Everything will come back at the right time, sir, don't worry. Your injury has been a shock for you.'

'You say a shell burst threw me quite a long way? I don't remember any shell burst, no sound, no impact. I have no reason to doubt it since you have seen it with your own eyes. But you see, I am not injured anywhere,' the leader said piteously, trying to indicate his body and limbs with his eyes. Then he continued, 'No shrapnel has pierced any part of my body. There is no blood.'

'Yes, there are no external injuries,' Ron agreed.

'You say I was thrown over a rock outcropping, isn't it? I don't remember any such thing. I probably lost my senses when the explosion threw me up and flung me down on the rocks. Tell me again about it, Ron.'

'It looked like a movie in slow motion,' Ron said. 'The mortar shells tore up the camp and the surrounding trees. The deep-throated rumble of big shells could be heard from time to time amidst the bursting of mortar shells. We were all cowering under an outcropping of rocks, trying to find shelter from the incessant shelling. People from the camp were running in small haphazard groups, trying to escape the mortar shelling and gunfire. You suddenly came running down the slope towards us. And then there was a huge shell burst—you were hurled up by the force and thrown out. You literally flew like a bird—before our eyes you flew and in slow motion, just like in the movies. It is really surprising that no shrapnel hit you. It was as if a blast of air released by the explosion picked you up and carried you away.'

They became silent for a few moments. June thought that the leader had again gone to sleep, or lost consciousness. But no, he had only kept his eyes closed for a few moments. She observed that the leader's eyes glistened quite abnormally. *Is he going to cry?* June wondered, and became uneasy. Ron also fidgeted a little. Then the leader composed himself and said in an even, sincere tone.

'I am so thankful to you, Ron, so thankful you took all the risk amidst such heavy shelling to climb up the hill to rescue me. You must have thought I was done for.'

'I did what I thought was my duty, sir. And yes, I was not sure till I examined you whether you were still alive. You were so still.'

'And when you examined me, what did you find?'

'I saw you were breathing, then I felt for your pulse, which was very rapid and thread-like. When I saw these signs I thought, thank God, you are at least alive. I also observed there was no apparent sign of any external injury. There was no blood anywhere.'

The leader asked, 'Then you brought me down? Was I very heavy, difficult to carry down?'

June knew that after gaining consciousness and getting back his ability to think and talk clearly, the leader liked to hear the story of the attack on the camp and his own rescue again and again.

'Honestly, sir, I don't remember. I don't remember how I brought you down. Whether I carried you or pulled you.

Other boys also helped, I could make that out towards the end.'

'Then? What did you do?'

'When we brought you down, we examined you for wounds. All of us were surprised to see that except for some superficial wounds on your elbows—where they had come into contact with the rocks—there were no cuts. I personally examined you thoroughly. I was really surprised to see that there was no bleeding. The only sign that your injury was serious was your unresponsiveness. You were totally unconscious.'

'You went up to the camp again? Why?'

'When at last the shelling ceased, I thought I must go and see the condition of the camp.'

'What did you find?'

'It was almost destroyed. Nobody was there. See, how many evacuation plans we made! Even held drills—mock drills—for it. But when the attack actually came, all our precautions failed, everything fell apart. Planned formations broke up and haphazard groups formed. Everybody retreated in great disarray. It was each one to himself.'

The leader sighed quite audibly. June thought it was one of the most tortured sagas she had ever heard. She also remembered two lines from somewhere that repeatedly came to her mind, 'Of best laid plans. Of mice and man.' She couldn't remember the beginning or the end so she added one line of her own—'best laid plans/ of mice and man/ always go up in smoke!' She wondered, *Should it be 'always'? Or would 'mostly' be more appropriate? Yes… 'mostly go up in smoke'. Were they not like a bunch of mice scurrying up a mound, tunnelling it and laying down stores of seeds and stolen grain for winter?* She thought of the camp they had built atop a high mountain, a camp that seemed so impregnable with its defence fortifications, ambush alleys, trenches and sentry posts—all to no avail, all gone in one attack!

Yes, she had also gone up to the camp when the shelling finally ceased. They dared to do so because darkness was approaching and it was not likely that the enemy would attack and try entering it then. She also felt that their future survival in that mountainous zone depended on going back to the camp and retrieving as many supplies as they could.

So, for the last time, they again scurried up the mountain like frightened, agitated little mice.

'Couldn't get much out from the camp, could you?' June became aware that the leader was asking Ron.

'Not much food,' Ron replied, 'No building was standing untouched in the camp. Many were burned, others simply collapsed in the shelling. We rolled down many items, but most were lost in the forest. We could bring a few bamboo poles and the canvas piece for your stretcher, plastic sheets, blankets, some warm clothes, ammunition and medicines and radio sets. How much can four persons bring?'

'Hm. Hm.' The leader nodded. 'You left before dark.'

'They started shelling again, even at night! They wanted to prevent us from regrouping after dark. This time the shelling was not very intense but it continued nearly the whole night. As soon as we could gather a fair amount of supplies, we left with you.'

June noticed that Ron didn't tell the leader that they were able to bring out two cooking pots, ropes and jerrycans of water.

'And you moved on and kept moving throughout the night?'

'We tried to move as far away and as quickly from that place as possible, but at night it was difficult to make out the way.'

8

'You shouldn't have done it, Ron, you shouldn't have brought me out like this. It's so impractical. I am putting you all into such trouble and risk,' the leader said loudly and clearly.

That day they had to cross a very narrow ledge on a rocky mountain face.

The stretcher swayed dangerously on the shoulders of the two stretcher-bearers. At times it seemed the leader would fall off the stretcher.

Everybody waited with bated breath, staring at the narrow path. There was a real danger that the swaying stretcher could drag the two carriers along with the leader down to the deep gorge below.

Slowly, they began to walk on it. When at last the bearers negotiated the ledge, the relief all around was palpable. Everyone just plopped down in the open area to rest.

It was then that the leader had spoken, 'This looks like madness to me.' He was fully conscious then. 'You shouldn't have brought me out.'

Ron just snorted in reply.

A little later, he told the leader in a lighter vein, 'This is one eventuality we have not thought of before, needing to carry a comrade on a stretcher over the mountains. We will have to put it in the training manual next time.'

Then he added, 'It is not that this is entirely new to us. We had to carry many of our injured friends before—but not like this.'

Everybody laughed, a reserved, strained laughter.

'I really mean it, Ron,' the leader said. 'You could have moved more easily if you didn't have to carry me. I am quite heavy, you know. I know you are taking this route only for me. Otherwise you could have gone down much earlier.'

'Those roads are no longer passable. You know that better than I do.'

The leader seemed pleased with Ron's remark.

He and Ron then started talking in undertones. They had again broken the journey after a short time, breaks happening more frequently lately. The stretcher-bearers would change shoulders every quarter or half-an-hour, depending on the terrain. And during the breaks, June would immediately come to the leader. She knew he was eating too little. Was it due to the shame he felt when he had to vacate his guts lying down on the stretcher? She had a suspicion that it was so. The proud man must have considered that to be the ultimate humiliation.

'You must eat a little more,' she would say. 'If you don't, you'll become even more weak. Since the morning, you have eaten only two biscuits. That won't do.'

The leader would smile then, as if he was amused by

June's concern. She would soften the biscuit by dipping it into the drinking water they carried in plastic jerrycans and the leader would eat it. The meagre stock of biscuits was reserved for the leader. Fortunately, they could fill their plastic jerrycans and water bottles at the innumerable streams that gurgled down the mountains, although many areas they crossed had no streams. They had plenty of water to last two to three days after each refill, but their food stock was really running low.

During daytime they had to eat their food raw, as the leader had strictly forbidden them to light fires in the day.

One day, when the leader and Ron started talking in hushed undertones, June realized that she should move away. She slowly rose and left them alone. She mumbled, 'Why didn't it occur to me to move away earlier? I am not thinking rationally any longer. My brain seems to be addled, every faculty is leaving me. I am talking to myself, like the leader does.'

Perhaps the food was to be blamed for it, the raw soaked beaten rice, the chira, was difficult to chew, sapping their strength and weakening them.

June thought, *I used to be such a sharp-witted person, a fast thinker, always ready with answers and repartee. Now my mind mostly remains blank, devoid of any thoughts. I've begun moving mechanically like a zombie, like a sleepwalker. And everything appears to be like a bad dream…nothing but a sleepwalker's dream…*

June felt a bitter fluid flooding her month and despite herself, she had to spit it out.

The nights had become really difficult for her. When, one by one, the others went to sleep, she alone would remain awake. The night sentries would change their duty at midnight but she would remain wide awake for a long time. Cocooned in her rough rug and curled up on the plastic sheet on the ground, she would try to fight off the biting cold and the demons that crowded her mind at that time.

And she became very frightened too.

She would imagine a wolf or a leopard suddenly materializing in the camp and attacking her, especially when she had to walk away from the camp to relieve herself behind bushes at night. Danger was not unknown to her. From wild elephants to armed men, from treacherous routes to mysterious fevers, encounters and chases—she had faced them all and survived. Nothing had dampened her spirit.

She knew that she had no fixed political belief or ideology. When she had joined the underground organization, it was not a thought-out decision or a result of any deep conviction. It just happened. She had floated in and settled down, carrying out her duties in great spirits and with good humour.

For the last two years, the people in the camp, especially the women, had a very routine, predictable and easy life. The camp was spacious, situated on a ridge on the mountain top. It had very formidable fortifications with sentry posts, ambush alleys and trenches. Beyond the borders of India, in a very sparsely populated mountainous area of Bhutan with rudimentary roads, it had felt safe there. Bhutan had practically no police or military presence to pose a threat to them.

There was no fighting, no immediate danger and no uncertainties for a long time. The work was easy—regular drills, physical training, marches, political classes (known as 'yawn' classes) and other camp work, such as cooking, fetching water and firewood, sentry duty in turns. There was a nursery school for the children of the camp inmates. It turned out that June was the only woman who had taught children (after her graduation), so she was put in charge of the school. It was a job she was very adept at. She took naturally to children and they to her.

It was a new world for her. Her past had almost ceased to exist for her, surviving only as a dim memory. The camp was the real world for her. It was like a village, a tight-knit community that felt like a cocoon of safety. She had the liberty to leave the camp also and visit the village nearby. She was encouraged by the leaders to visit the households, mingle with the women and children as a part of their public relations exercise but she was asked to keep her eyes and ears open, to act as a barometer to gauge the atmosphere, to decipher what the villagers' views about the camp were.

Of course, she had heard discussions in the camp about the possibility of attacks on their camp, of hostilities, but that kind of talk didn't affect her, was of no concern to her. Those problems didn't belong to her world at all.

Her world. What had been her world like?

Her life in the camp was like a dream, something alien, unreal, not tangible, and her present too, drifting through the mountains, was the same.

She suddenly saw a vision of herself in other people's eyes, a happy, bubbly woman taking part in different camp activities, activities planned to keep everybody busy— parading, marching with a cap on her head, shouting slogans, practising bayonet charges.

She thought, *Am I really that girl? Am I?*

She had never liked the mountains. She even disliked the low hills where her childhood had been spent. Was it the unevenness, the high and low terrain, the winding paths up and down?

She liked her flat village situated in a rolling rice bowl through which a small beautiful river lazily wound its way. She remembered how she could glide on the village pathways so effortlessly!

In the camp, more than the height and the unevenness, she hated the pinching cold. As long as she was in the camp it was bearable because there was always the warmth of conversation and the fires that were lit. But in this bleak mountainside where they had halted, the cold was like a curse. She felt the cold had been sent specifically for her as a punishment for her wayward life! No one else seemed to be as bothered about the cold. They merely pulled their jacket lapels up and their caps down and went on working. It was she and only she who suffered because of it, sometimes making her life a nightmare.

9

RON HAD TOLD the leader that he had felt relieved only on the evening of the third day after he, the leader, had regained consciousness. 'Only when you drank water normally, ate some gruel and began to talk normally,' he said.

The leader said, 'I have no recollection of my period of unconsciousness, or even about the events that caused it. It was a total blank, until I discovered I was riding on a stretcher carried by two of our boys and moving through a mountainside. You know, when I came to my senses fully, I found the whole occurrence so weird that I couldn't believe it was really happening. So weird, so strange!'

Ron had nodded his head then.

'It was after I regained my consciousness that I became aware that I could not move my legs. It was in the morning, yes, in the morning—I could feel that my legs were not obeying me...'

'I know,' Ron had replied. 'But I think it is a temporary phenomenon, sir.'

'You do? But I think I have become a paraplegic. Even my arms feel leaden and weak,' the leader said in an urgent tone.

'No, it's not like that, sir,' replied Ron, trying to be encouraging.

'When I realized I was paralysed, I tried to scream, but no sound came out of my mouth. Do you know how I felt? An all-enveloping dread and all-consuming rage at the same time. It was rage, dread, bitter helplessness and misery—all rolled into one.'

'I can understand, but sir, you mustn't look at it negatively.'

The leader paid no attention to what Ron was trying to say. He continued talking.

'Whenever we had a short break and the stretcher was put down, the girl, what's her name? June? She would bring me water which I would refuse. One day, she spoke to me softly, "Your legs are not moving," she told me in a matter-of-fact way, "not moving at all. I shall massage them and warm them with hot stones and they will soon get better." Moving her hand under the blankets, she touched my toes and massaged them. I looked at her—her eyes were bright and reassuring. Even though I had my doubts, I wanted to believe her. "If only I could have some oil," she said. "I would have warmed it and massaged your legs with warm oil. That would have helped more. Now I will have to massage without oil." From the movement of her shoulders, I could make out that she was already working on my legs under the blanket. Only, I felt nothing.'

Ron felt a little uneasy at the leader's talk. He wished to cut it short, change the subject. He said, 'Don't worry, sir. You'll feel less weak as time goes on.'

The leader paid no attention to him.

'Impotent rage, isn't that what they call it? Impotent rage. Oh, the misery of that rage made me cry. Tears welled up in my eyes and I cried silently and unashamedly. I felt very helpless.'

Ron snorted in response, not knowing what to say.

'My back and shoulders are sore from the constant friction with the stretcher's canvas. Imagine yourself constantly riding on a stretcher carried on the shoulders of two young men, like a corpse on a bier on the way to the funeral.'

Ron felt very restless at the leader's words. He began fidgeting but didn't want to interrupt the leader any more. Perhaps he would feel better if he could unburden himself by expressing his misery.

'Probably it's no use lamenting over my helplessness,' the leader said. 'Life sometimes feels like a bleak emptiness, like the void after a pleasureless masturbation, tinged with the bitter after-taste of frustration.'

Ron was shocked to hear the leader talking in such language. He stood up and said firmly, 'You shouldn't worry too much, sir. Your nerves are in a state of shock, totally numbed by the impact of the blast. Nerves take a notoriously long time to recover, but recover they will. I am sure of it.'

'You sound so reassuring, like a specialist doctor. I can only hope you are right.'

After that conversation with Ron, the leader went into a bout of melancholia, kept mostly to himself and talked very little. His usual banter with the stretcher-bearers during the journey practically ceased.

The next day, the leader craned his neck to see the skyline, the mountains. The scenery looked very familiar to him, yes, too familiar. He became agitated, grit his teeth and suddenly shouted, 'Stop, I say stop!'

The stretcher-bearers were startled. They halted immediately and June rushed to his side. He ignored their enquiring looks and commanded, 'Call Ron immediately!'

Ron came running. The leader said impatiently, 'Where do you think we are heading? Aren't we heading north? North or northeast, to be exact? Aren't we going in the opposite direction?'

'Yes, sir.'

'And what do you have to say about that, Ron? I suddenly had this feeling that we are not going in the right direction. I tried to be sure, doubly sure. It's difficult to be sure when you lie face-up in a stretcher. After repeated attempts to find our bearings, I was sure we are heading the wrong way.'

The leader's voice was authoritative, like the real commander he was. In deference to him, Ron stood at attention and replied in a formal way.

'Sir, we couldn't take any of the paths down because all of them are totally sealed by the enemy. We couldn't even venture that way. The main attack on our camp came by the two southern main paths. Even the last southward band over the mountains was sealed. So I decided to take the longest route, going north first then turning east.'

'And cross the big river?'

'Yes, sir.'

'Do you realize that the river can't be crossed, except by the hanging bridge? And the narrow hanging bridge is high up in the gorge?'

'Yes, sir.'

'Well?' the leader waited expectantly.

'Yes, sir, we shall somehow have to cross the bridge.'

'And the enemy will mow us all down as we cross.'

'I expect that area to be relatively peaceful, sir. We hardly ever use that road. It is unlikely to be guarded. That's why I wanted to attempt that route. Moreover, there are quite a few villages on the way. Once we can cross the river, there won't be any problem, sir.'

The leader remained silent for some time, probably realizing the merit of Ron's arguments. 'I know these areas very well,' he finally said, and then went on in a roundabout way. 'I have travelled over these mountain ranges more than any local man. It started more than five years ago, when I combed this area with my groups and some guides. Do you know why? We were looking for suitable places to build our camp. Since then I have been regularly scouring these areas for newer paths, hideouts, places to build storage depots, satellite defence camps. I know these areas like the back of my hand.'

'Yes, sir.' Ron stood at attention before the leader and the other boys stood like statues.

'I understand your point, Ron,' the leader said, 'You have some solid reasons. Now everything will depend on our ability to cross that hanging bridge. To me it seems quite impossible at the present moment.'

Everybody waited expectantly to hear what the leader would say, but he remained silent for some time. He was trying to remember what he had seen the last time he was in the area. A vague picture of the bridge floated before his eyes. Yes, yes, he had seen a guard house at the end of the bridge. It was a flat-roofed construction, like the nondescript stone houses in the mountains, with small square cubbyhole windows. Yes, he remembered a low stone wall surrounding the guard house, walls of a comfortable height for a gunman to rest his rifle on the top of the wall and fire. He didn't remember whether the guard house belonged to the police or military forces.

'I remember seeing a guard house at the end of the bridge,' the leader said. 'It's likely that it will be manned. They may abandon their posts after a month or so, but not now.'

The leader's apprehensions turned out to be valid.

He asked Ron to go for a scouting trip. And leaving the rest of the party in a safe densely forested area, Ron and his companion crossed the ridge of the mountain and went down to see the bridge.

June was very thankful for the break. She sorely needed it as the journey on the mountain trail had really drained her. The leader also seemed to be happy to have a break from the constant swaying on the stretcher. He slept most of the time. June also made him lie on his sides and massaged his back.

'You are looking for bed sores, aren't you?' he asked.

'We have to look out for any eventuality,' she replied firmly. 'It is to prevent any pressure sores that I am making you lie on your side. You can't do so while we are moving.'

Ron and his companion returned the next evening. Everybody waited expectantly to hear what they had discovered.

Ron stood in front of the leader and said, 'As you guessed, the bridge is well fortified, sir. There are sandbag enclosures on both ends with trenches and guard posts. They are probably afraid that we may blow up the bridge.'

The leader nodded slowly. Everybody looked dejected.

All routes of retreat, of escaping, were sealed.

There was no way but to go down to the plains of Assam.

Their food stock was fast running out and they knew that food was scarce in the mountains. It was to avoid the danger of starving that they came to the decision to change track.

10

THE WHOLE PARTY trudged over the mountain tracks, trying to remain under the cover of trees as much as they could. Occasionally, however, they had to travel through bare areas and exposed paths. According to Ron's instructions, the party had placed leafy tree branches on their caps, shoulders and even waists as camouflage.

June was amused to hear such an order at first, but she also dutifully put leaves and branches on her hat and over her knapsack and held a long leafy frond. Then on a stony, winding stretch she could see that the group looked like small trees on the move! From a distance it would be very difficult to spot them as people.

Ron really knows his job, she had to admit to herself.

During the rest break, the leader had asked Ron about the food situation.

'We are on strict rationing, sir,' Ron had replied. 'And I think,' June heard Ron saying a little reluctantly, 'with a major meal a day and two small helpings in between of dry, puffed rice, our stocks can stretch for another three or four days.'

June could see that the leader was deeply worried as

was Ron. Their faces were expressionless, like masks. They remained silent for a long time.

'Food is the most difficult thing to find in the mountains,' the leader said softly.

'I know,' Ron replied 'we shall have to do something quickly.'

'Yes, but what?'

'Send a scouting party forward to look for food.'

They fell silent again.

June felt the air had become thick with a palpable anxiety. She was lying on the ground, within earshot of the stretcher laid on the ground over its four supporting tripods. She closed her eyes, refusing to worry about food and soon dozed off. She didn't hear Ron say, 'The lack of food is affecting the strength of our boys. You may have noticed how frequently the rest breaks take place. At night the night sentries doze off at their posts. Look at June—she sank into sleep the moment she hit the ground.'

Suddenly— they heard the drone of helicopters!

A pair of helicopters came into view from the east. They were flying quite high and silhouetted against the blue sky, looked like two huge, angry hornets. Then, like two kites, they dived down, coming close to the tree lines of the mountains opposite.

The leader looked up, and said, 'They have not stopped their hunt, as you can see. Even after so many days, they are still scanning the mountainside.'

The group was well under the tree cover when the helicopters appeared, but everyone crouched down on the ground and the stretcher was placed on the low tripods. From time to time the helicopters disappeared from view and then reappeared again. It was clear that they were searching for something.

'We must move to thicker jungle,' Ron suddenly barked. 'The trees and the undergrowth here are not dense. Move fast to that patch where there is thick jungle.' Ron gestured to the stretcher-bearers, 'Double quick,' he hissed.

The leader didn't say anything.

The party immediately moved to a patch of forest with a dense canopy.

As it was a slanting ground, the stretcher was precariously perched. To steady it, one end was placed on the ground and the other end jammed into a tree trunk and lashed securely, thus keeping it horizontal.

Then everybody took up positions on the ground.

'If they come by our left side we are protected well by the mountain face and on our right by the foliage cover in the slopes,' Ron told the leader, 'but if they fly directly overhead we are a little exposed there.' Then he barked out an order. 'Nobody should shoot at the helicopters, even if they fly quite close. Nobody should move or take any action. Is that clear?'

There was a murmur of assent from the boys.

June was surprised that it had taken them less than a minute to move to their positions. She observed the leader. He also nodded when Ron gave the order.

And they waited for the helicopters to come.

After some time they heard the drone of the helicopters, which gradually increased in intensity.

'Nobody is to move. Stay frozen where you are,' Ron again hissed out.

June felt her heart beating faster. She lay very still. She saw Ron quickly breaking some leafy twigs from the undergrowth and putting them over the stretcher to cover the leader.

The helicopters reached quite near and their drone had become a deafening roar—through the roar, the clatter of rotating blades could be heard.

They are too close, June thought.

In the next moment, the helicopters roared overhead, a little to their right. But then they passed the hiding place and the drone became faint.

'Do not rise,' Ron ordered. 'Stay on the ground. No movements.'

And sure enough, after a little while they could hear the helicopters again.

They are coming back! June thought. *Why? Did they see us from the sky, spot something suspicious? They are sure to open fire then.*

She closed her eyes, only to open them immediately.

The drone of the helicopters came nearer and the sound of the engines resounded again. It was possible that only one helicopter had come back, and was returning to join its companion. June saw Ron slowly rising from the ground and going to the edge of the clump of trees, trying to make out where the helicopters had gone.

'Have they left?' the leader asked.

'Looks like they have gone,' June said. The leader was

half hidden by the branches Ron had put over him. June got up from the ground, went near the stretcher and slowly removed the branches. The leader looked very pale.

Ron returned hurriedly from his look-out.

'It seems the helicopters are coming back again this way,' he said. 'We must be doubly careful. Either they suspect something or they are returning by the same path.'

He then looked all around, instructed some of the boys to take cover more carefully and came back to the stretcher. June started putting back the leafy branches over the leader again.

Soon the drone of the helicopters could be heard again. But this time they stayed at a distance, flying over the narrow valley below. They slowly disappeared in the direction they had come from but the droning vibration remained in their ears for a long time.

They all rose from the ground, dusted themselves and prepared to continue their journey.

11

THEY WERE CROSSING a treeless hillock on the mountain road at that time. On the right side of this path was the craggy mountain face towering high above the path, the left side an open area. And the whole panoramic view of the mountains floated under a pale blue sky. Several formations of mountain ridges, each successively higher, could be seen.

June observed that the leader had turned his head towards the mountains and was looking at them intently. He had been mostly silent since his last conversation with Ron.

'Hey!' the leader suddenly shouted out, his voice quivering with excitement.

June was startled. So were the stretcher-bearers.

She saw that the leader was trying to raise his head as much as he could.

'Hey, look there, at the twin peaks!' the leader shouted.

He indicated the mountains in front of them. It was obvious he was trying to think hard, to understand the import of the scene before him. The twin peaks! They appeared before his eyes like an apparition.

I must have been looking at them, but without recognizing

them, he thought. *They must have been there for quite some time before my eyes. I was looking at them, but somehow they didn't register.*

'Hey!' he shouted again.

The stretcher-bearers came to a stop. Everybody had stopped in their tracks, June reached the stretcher and placed her hand over the leader's. Ron came running from the front.

'The twin peaks,' the leader pointed them out to Ron with his head.

'Yes, sir,' Ron appeared puzzled.

'Our problems are over, Ron.'

'Sir?'

'Don't you hear me? Our problems are over!' he shouted in an excited voice. 'Our problems are over. We only have to reach the base of those twin peaks, and ascend up a little. Let us go there as fast as we can.'

June looked at the peaks before her. Yes, the nearest mountain rose to twin peaks, one a little taller than the other as if the mountain top was divided into two. She saw that Ron was intently looking at the peaks too.

Everybody was silent. June saw that they were all looking furtively at each other, as if to figure out whether the leader was speaking in a delirium. She had also fleetingly thought that. She looked at Ron. Was he mentally calculating the distance and the time it would take for the party to reach the peaks? He was probably trying to figure out the way to them, using his binoculars.

The leader then spoke in a triumphant voice, 'I will now let you into a secret.'

'Yes, sir,' Ron lowered his binoculars and came near the leader.

The leader looked at him with bright, shining eyes.

'Ron, do you know what is there at the base of the twin mountain peaks?' The leader spoke in a quivering voice. 'There is food, medicines, other provisions, even some arms.'

Ron didn't reply but waited for the leader to speak.

'Of course, you haven't been told about it. How could you know?' the leader said slowly. 'There is a cave there, a little way up from the base. It is a fairly large cave with two irregular chambers and a crazy twisted exit. There is even a wet patch where water drips and collects in a large pool inside—water will be no problem. It flows out through the exit and collects in another small pool outside…' The leader's voice faltered, possibly due to the exhaustion caused by his excitement.

'Sounds like a natural hideout,' Ron said.

'It is a natural hideout. I discovered it two years back and I thought we must build a fallback store. An attack on our main camp was not entirely unforeseen.'

Ron nodded.

'I got the clearance from higher-ups and slowly built it up in a couple of trips. Last time I visited, it was about six months ago. There is rice, oil and other food too—dal, biscuits, onions, garlic and corn. Food remains fresh in this cold climate for a long time.'

His words caused a stir among the group. June could make out that everybody was mentally ready to go to the cave.

'Let's start!' Ron barked out an order. And the motley group started moving….

June looked at the members of her group. She could see a new spring to the boys' steps. The thought of hot, cooked food, of a good square meal, had brought new energy to them.

Will there be dried chillies there? June thought, a little ashamed of her thoughts. But the leader had talked about a cave full of food, hadn't he?

She dreaded caves. Those dark, damp, smelly dungeons often crowded with bats.

She tried to shake off her dread.

The twin peaks shimmered under the blue sky before her, like a mirage.

June tried to keep her mind blank, tried to banish all thoughts.

While they were going forward, one of the boys of the group approached Ron and started walking along with him. Ron could sense that he wanted to ask something but was not able to muster up the required courage to do so. So he asked, 'What is it, Pradip?'

The boy hesitated for a few seconds, then asked, 'Is there really such a cave, sir?'

'Why? Why do you doubt it?

'Well, sir,' the boy said, 'our leader is quite ill. The shock has not completely worn off. It is shell-shock, sir, I have read about it. Shell-shocked people can imagine things. They can make mistakes too.'

Ron nodded.

'It will take us a minimum of two days to reach the place with the stretcher, sir, otherwise we could have reached it in one day. We are very low in rations. It will hardly last us two days even with the strictest rationing'.

'What do we have in stock?'

'Some rice, some rice flakes and dal. The dal remained because we have practically given up cooking.'

'Anything else?'

'Some biscuits, four bars of chocolate and two packets of glucose powder, and sir…'

'Yes?'

'If we reach the cave and find that there is no food, we will be in dire straits, sir.'

'Yes, I know,' Ron said softly, 'Let's go and find out first.' He felt a sudden surge of affection for the boy walking by his side. *Where has this fresh-faced boy come from?* Ron wondered. *I must make it a point to know all the members of our present group intimately. Fate has thrown us together and we shall have to negotiate our way out of this present situation with each other's support.*

Then he asked Pradip, 'What other alternative can you think of?'

The boy fumbled. He apparently hadn't thought about anything concrete. Ron looked at him, wondering how old he was. Twenty-five, twenty-six at the most. The lower part of his forehead was quite dark but the upper part was of a pale hue. He had removed his regulation cap and was wringing it nervously in his hands. He seemed ready to take the risk of getting through the enemy pickets into the plains of Assam. Most of the boys were experienced at this and had often made forays in the past to get food supplies, medicines and other goods from Assam, evading the police and army pickets always there, ready to hunt and gun them down.

Now, with open hostilities on, the odds against them were much more.

Ron knew the boys were dreaming of plates of hot steaming rice with dal, vegetable curry and raw green chillies that they usually got after entering the plains of Assam. Ron himself felt his mouth watering at the thought of hot food. He looked at Pradip's serious face and smiled.

'It will be best if we can sit out this crisis in the cave, sir,' Pradip said tentatively. 'Within a few days, the enemy guard will be less vigilant and our leader will also get well.'

Ron nodded, then added, 'I only hope that there is enough food in the cave.'

'Even if there is some food to last us a few days—I will ration it in such a way that it will last longer. We can add to it. I will try to get wild potatoes, roots and vegetables—and I know how to set traps for wild animals.'

'You do?' Ron was happy to hear that.

'You know, I have even eaten rats! Rodents as big as cats and even bats.'

'I, too, have eaten rats in Arunachal. And frogs too. Frog legs are like tender chicken legs.'

'Yes, sir, if we can go down to the valley, we may get many edible things there, and game too.'

'But you won't be able to shoot. The sound of gunshots

travels a long distance in these areas—it echoes in rocky mountains.'

The boy agreed, then added, 'We'll be able to trap small game and birds.'

'Let's hope so,' Ron said. 'Some cooked meat will be really welcome…'

12

'WE'LL TAKE JUST one more day to reach the cave, sir,' Ron told the leader in a happy tone. 'We are nearly there.'

'Yes,' the leader replied gravely. 'We would have reached it a long time ago if only I could have walked. But I have hampered you all with my illness.'

'You shouldn't keep on saying that, sir,' Ron protested sincerely. 'While we were on the move, we couldn't take as good care of you as we should have. Now once we reach the cave, you can rest and eat better. Your health will improve.'

'I know how difficult it is to carry a stretcher. I am having fits of depression you know, Ron. Really, I am telling you, it's difficult to fight depressing feelings.'

He paused for a while. Ron waited for the leader to continue.

'Riding helplessly on the shoulders of young boys, I feel so guilty and frustrated at times that I want to die. At one point where we were crossing that narrow stony area with the deep crevice on the side, when they were carrying the stretcher on the narrow ledge with great difficulty, I really wanted to jump into the gorge. Then I realized I couldn't move on my own so how could I do that? I felt so helpless that I wanted to cry. And had I moved, the two boys carrying me would also have fallen to their death…' his voice trailed off.

'You mustn't talk like that. It will only hinder your recovery.' Then to divert the leader, he asked. 'How did you first discover the caves, sir? Tell us about that.'

'You may try to divert my attention from such depressing things as death, Ron, but the truth remains that one can't escape it.'

He smiled at June, who was listening to him with a solemn, anxious expression. The leader continued, 'I know I am paralysed, I don't know how much I will recover, if at all. In such situations, it's only natural that people will talk about death, think about it, but the main point is that you have to have the strength to overcome such negative thoughts. Don't I know that, Ron? But when you are physically incapable it is so difficult to keep up your spirits.'

'Humans have always fought and overcome adversity.' It was all Ron could manage to say.

The leader let out a hollow laugh.

'There are certain situations where you can't win, however much you try. It is better if you can accept it. Then possibly, you can think of a new way to overcome depression.'

'That's a positive way of looking at things,' Ron said.

'What were you asking me, Ron? About the cave?'

'Yes, sir. Everybody is eager to know about it. Why did you go to the base of the twin peaks?'

'It happened totally by chance. I stumbled upon it!'

Everybody gathered around the stretcher to hear the story.

'We had a guide at that time. He told us that there was a high plateau with a stream flowing through it in this area, which was ideal for a campsite. We searched for it, but couldn't find it. Instead, I found the cave during that expedition.'

June observed the faces of all the boys around the stretcher. Some had disbelief writ on them.

The leader continued his story. 'Do you know? The guide refused to enter the cave, saying that there would be ghosts and spirits inside—bad air! Yes, he called it bad air.'

'And you entered it?'

'It was musty and smelly when I first entered. Despite that, it was quite clean and dry. Surprisingly, there were no bats inside, possibly because of the altitude. I explored it thoroughly with my flashlight.'

'Was it dark?'

'All caves are dark.'

'Then what happened?'

'Immediately it struck me—this would be a great hideout. Different possibilities came to my mind. It can serve as a storehouse, a fallback store, a magazine, as a redoubt and what not. It would have also made a good command post, only it was way off from the main routes.'

'And ultimately you chose the first one.'

'That came much later. But immediately after coming out from the cave, I told the guide that he was right. The cave definitely felt haunted. Surely it was full of bad air and demons and monsters must be cavorting in it. One shouldn't go near such places.'

'What did the guide say?'

'The guide was relieved that I corroborated his fear. He was a happy man.'

'When did you stock it?'

'Much later. I diverted some of the supplies meant for the camp and had them brought there. I used a group of trusted boys. I think there are some small arms and ammunition in the cave as well as blankets and medicines.'

'But would the food have stayed all right for so long?'

'It does in these cold and dry areas. The food items are in airtight polythene and sealed containers. They should preserve well.'

Everybody was hanging on to the words of the leader.

'There must be a radio set there,' the leader said. 'What I don't remember now is whether it is an old type with batteries.'

'That will be great!' Ron said enthusiastically. 'We couldn't bring our main set because the person carrying it was blown up in the first shelling. The small set that we could manage to bring out was blown up in the first encounter we had. It saved the life of the boy who was carrying it.'

'In a way it is good,' the leader said with a chuckle. 'We are having to maintain a radio silence out of necessity. If we had the radio on, the enemy could have heard us. Now our friends and foes alike don't know whether we are alive or not. Under the present circumstances, don't you think it's the most desirable situation?' The leader gave a hollow laugh.

June could sense that everybody was fully convinced

of the existence of the cave with its food store. They shed their indifference and had become animated and happy. *It's so comforting to be able to believe in something,* she thought, happy that the ordeal of travelling over the mountainside was coming to an end at last. She looked at Ron. He also had a satisfied look. His perpetually mask-like serious face had dissolved into joy!

'I think I will ask for a hot meal to be prepared today,' he told the leader. 'The last one before we reach the cave.'

'Do you think we should light a fire?'

'The boys are adept at it. Let them have a hot meal tonight. They need it.'

'Okay, if you think so.' The leader didn't sound very happy.

Ron didn't pay any attention to him. He got up, called Pradip and told him to issue the rations for a good hot meal.

Pradip looked a little uncertain, hesitating a little. Then a smile lit up his face. Soon there was excitement at the campsite. Ron could feel the anticipation floating in the patch of forest they were in. Later, he was glad to see the satisfaction of the boys as they ate their frugal cooked meal that afternoon.

And soon after that, the cold came rolling down the mountain slopes into the campsite.

The valley-like depression at the base of the twin peaks was slowly blanketed by a bank of fog from the mountains. Then slowly, darkness descended, engulfing the whole campsite in gloom.

13

FINDING THE CAVE was no easy job.

The leader seemed to have lost his bearings. Twice he led the party in the wrong direction. Everyone was helpless since it was only he who knew about the cave.

The leader also seemed to be greatly disturbed.

After two failed attempts, he made everyone stop in one place, and gazed at the twin peaks through field glasses for a long time. Everybody was silent. June observed that they even stopped looking at each other.

'It will be here, somewhere quite nearby, believe me,' the leader mumbled aloud. 'We will find it soon.'

The spot he was looking at was not really the base of the twin peaks. They were still far off. However, the ground started to incline steeply from that point to a very tall stony ridge, above which was a plateau-like elevation. The ridge ultimately went up and merged into the base of the twin peaks.

'I am confused because I have not been able to see the way normally. Lying on a stretcher makes it difficult to see things as they really are,' the leader said.

June had to agree that he had a point there.

This time the leader took them to the opposite direction. Soon they reached a dry nullah, strewn with huge boulders.

'This area looks as if the tongue of a glacier left it a long time ago!' Ron said.

'Well, we are nearing the cave—it's not very far off,' the leader said.

After some time, they came to a place where there was a stone wall on one side and a rocky open space on the other. The leader made them stop there. He looked at the stone wall, the open space and the mountains long and hard. 'It ought to be here,' he mumbled.

He said, 'One of you must climb up to the stony ledge and find the depression through which one can climb up.'

Kumbang immediately put his knapsack down and scurried up the stony elevation like a mountain goat. He soon disappeared from view. Surely there was some kind of stony platform above. Everybody waited below with bated breath. After a few moments, Kumbang appeared above the ledge. He shouted, 'The cave is here, the cave is here! Its opening has been covered with branches and stone. It is here!'

A loud murmur rose from the group below.

Lifting the stretcher up was not an easy job. Luckily the stone wall below the ledge was not very high.

'The cave mouth cannot be seen from the gully below,' the leader said. 'It can be seen only when snow fills the gully.'

Ron ordered everyone not to enter the cave. He had the branches and stones removed from the cave mouth and

June saw that he took both the torchlight and the rifle in hand! *What is he expecting inside?* she asked herself. *Some stranger or a big black Himalayan bear? Or a leopard with cubs? Or wolves, maybe?* She was no longer afraid of them now. A wolf pack nearby would be welcome.

Ron came out with a smile on his face. He had found neither intruders nor poisonous gas inside the cave. With a hurrah, the group then rushed in, leaving the leader in his stretcher on its tripod stands outside.

'There is lots of food and blankets here!' Kumbang shouted.

Then before June and Ron's eyes, the leader closed his eyes and went off to sleep. They looked at each other. Ron said, 'He was really very worried at not being able to find the cave at first. The tension had drained him. It's good that he's getting some rest. Please cover him with blankets…'

Ron then went inside the cave.

June kept sitting there near the leader. The afternoon sun felt very pleasant. She thought, *I should have felt happy like the others at finding the cave. Though nobody talked much about it, everyone was really worried that there might be no cave at the base of the twin mountains. I should have been happy, relieved, but why is it that I am so indifferent? It is not right, it's not normal. I must be more active.* She got up, then went to the mouth of the cave and peered inside. The boys were energetically cleaning it. In the sunlight at the mouth of the cave, fine dust particles floated like a shimmering veil. Ron was directing Pradip and Kumbang, pointing to a spot at a height. It was probably where the leader would stay. June moved away from the cave entrance.

Suddenly she had a strong urge to pee. She looked around, but couldn't see a suitable place. She realized that she would have to do the needful before the boys came out from the cave. She went towards a stony ledge which led away from the cave from where it wound around the ridge of the mountain face. From that end, the cave mouth couldn't be seen. She chose a spot and relieved herself there, then hurried back to the leader. He was still sleeping peacefully.

Then she looked around. In the front of the ledge, the plateau descended gently into a heavily wooded area full of pines, deodars and other conifers. Beyond it rose the mountains, tier after tier, and in the distance the magnificent snow-capped peaks of the eastern Himalayas. What struck June immediately was the eerie silence that pervaded the area.

Ron came out of the cave and dusted himself. He had his binoculars in hand. He looked at the leader, nodded to June, then went along the ledge. He stopped in the middle, put the binoculars to his eyes and scanned the horizon. He stood at the ledge for a long time, then sat down with his legs dangling from the edge, never removing the binoculars from his eyes. He was looking at the surroundings with a clinical eye, knowing they had to stay in the cave for a few days. The leader and the whole group needed rest. He himself was also feeling weak.

Then he started thinking about the past.

It had been a long time—three decades. A lifetime really. The entire state of Assam had passed through a series of upheavals then. The whole of society was in a flux. There was a mass agitation against the infiltration of foreign nationals. It was preceded by a flow of leftist ideas and debates. Not only that, the left parties had made significant electoral gains too. Was it not this situation, which had frightened the landowning middle classes into looking for a nationalist agenda? The issue of the influx of foreign nationals came in handy and the repression of the nationalist movement led to the birth of the insurgency. It was a topic they had debated long and hard about at the initial stage of their organization.

Deep in his thoughts, Ron put the binoculars on his lap, but kept sitting on the ledge a little slumped forward. June was sure he was not looking at the magnificent mountain ranges in front of him. He seemed to be oblivious to his surroundings.

Ron was reflecting that the whole turbulent period had been an intellectually stimulating time when people endlessly debated different issues. *It was as if people were in constant arguments—in each house, the dining rooms, verandas, community prayer halls, markets, bazaars, in all platforms of debate, people endlessly talked politics. It was through this discourse that people became politically conscious.* He knew he himself was a political product of those particular times.

Ron looked up from his sitting position at the mountain range and the sky. The blue sky was becoming paler with the advancing afternoon and the breeze already carried a suggestion of cold. He looked towards the leader and June, who was arranging the blanket over him.

Ron felt a sense of loneliness creeping over him.

The cave was located in the spur of the mountain, a massive stony outcropping which rose quite steeply and went up to the base of the massive twin peaks for a considerable distance. Below the ledge where he was sitting was a sloping plateau-like area dotted with large boulders and scarred by crevices. In the soil, dwarf plants had taken root and many had broken out into small multicoloured flowers, islands of colour against a grey stone background. Clumps of tall conifers, a scene not uncommon in the Himalayas, added an intense green.

14

A LITTLE STRIP of silicon had brought her to this world! A tiny strip called the mobile sim card. In a sudden, inexplicable way it had carried June from one world to the other.

She had been working in a private school, then, in a northeastern oil town. She was happy and comfortable working in that small school, teaching tiny tots to read and write, to sing and dance, to play! She had created a neat, peaceful home in the little two-roomed house in the compound with the school ayah. Now, looking back at those carefree days, she sometimes wondered if those days had really existed. Or had they been just a dream?

Those memories appeared to be fast fading away!

During her stay in the mountain camp and during the journey—snippets of old memories came back to her like a disjointed jumble of images.

And it was at that time, yes, at that time, a man from her past suddenly reappeared in her life. Like an apparition from her misty past! The town was quite far away from the village where she was born. It was after her mother's death that her mother's cousin took her away to stay with her in the little hill town.

'I am much older than your mother,' her mother's cousin had said, 'but I developed such a close relationship with your mother, Niru. It's not that I used to meet her frequently. Before my marriage she visited us for some days. Quite a young girl she was then, still in frocks. Your granny had for some reason brought her to our home. My marriage was being arranged at that time—the negotiations were going on. And I remember it was then that I developed a strong liking for Niru. It was a liking, a love, which I can't explain even today! I never loved even my own brothers and sisters so much. Niru had very large eloquent eyes. She didn't talk much, but her eyes were expressive. Have you ever observed your mother's eyes?'

'Yes, she had large eyes.' June said, 'but they frequently brimmed over with tears.'

'She shed tears throughout her life,' her aunt said. 'She used to follow me everywhere with her doe eyes. Never let me out of her sight. The very first night she came to our house, she came clutching a shawl to sleep with me. She waited silently near me, didn't say a word. After the first night, she never left me again. After getting into bed at night—oh, how she would talk non-stop!'

And from then onward, her mother had developed a close bond with her older cousin which lasted through all the ups and downs of life. She remembered that when her mother became seriously ill, she asked for her cousin, who had arrived post-haste just a day before her death. June remembered how distraught she was.

This affectionate aunt of June was married to a

government employee who was posted in the hill town. He worked as a chief clerk dealing with files relating to government contracts, supplies and purchases. The jolly, efficient man was liked by all the government officials and local politicians. Her aunt had three children, a boy and two girls, all three of them older than June. Her aunt liked to entertain guests and kept an open house for all her relatives from both sides—hers and her husband's.

Her aunt had told June, 'You have seen our home, it's like a public place. People are welcome to stay with us for as long as they like.'

'I know, every day you have two or three guests at meals, sometimes more,' June said

'Yes, what's the big deal in giving someone a ladleful of rice? You don't feed them fish or meat every day, do you? They get whatever we cook for ourselves at home. The main thing is to give them affection. Your uncle has constructed that long thatched house outside for guests since this small hill town doesn't have a hotel worth the name. And the people who come here don't usually have the money to stay the night in a hotel. When they leave for home, many ask for the bus fare back home from your uncle. Some young men come in search of the elusive government jobs with such hope! They knock at the offices, at the doors of politicians and officers, but most of them have to go back empty-handed. That's what I have seen all these days. We let them stay for a few days—at least they have a place to lie down at night in this lonely hill town.'

Her aunt's daughter had once told June, 'There is no

use talking to Ma about her guests. People tell her their sob stories and Ma melts. Our father is busy the whole day in office and in the evening goes straight to play bridge, coming back only at dinner time. We all are busy so what would Ma do all day long? She busies herself with the guests so we have stopped complaining.'

Then one day a young man turned up. He was related to June's uncle and stayed for a long time. He didn't sleep in the long thatched house meant for guests, but in a portion of the back veranda covered with wooden planks and converted into a small room with a tiny window. He enrolled himself in the government technical institute in the town.

Her aunt's two daughters lived in their own world. They displayed a royal disdain for the procession of young men who came as guests, but were adept at finding out the background of each one. How they did it was a mystery to June. Later she discovered that the domestic help was the main source of information. At night they would sit on their beds and indulge in juicy gossip about the guests. June also became a part of their gossip circle.

The young man—Joy—was no exception. But Joy became a good friend of their brother within a short time, which annoyed June, who worshipped the elder brother from a distance. She could never stomach the fact that this new young man talked so much with her second cousin. She was jealous.

She told her cousins, 'What does that lout talk about with your elder brother? He is always whispering into your brother's ears! Why such closeness? His motives can't be good, whispering every time as if telling a secret!'

The sisters readily agreed. They also didn't like Joy. Although he seemed to have captured their brother totally, they chose to ignore Joy completely. June couldn't go to such lengths though she would have liked to do the same. She at least talked to Joy civilly.

June tried to remember what Joy had been like at the time.

There was a special character in his voice, June said to herself. *He had probably tried to imitate a popular film star, giving a special lilt to his voice in an effort to dramatize it.* The voice floated into her memory. Also, she remembered the cutting comments her cousins made about him, calling him a village bumpkin behind his back. All the girls were jealous of him because of his close friendship with their brother, but were careful not to let their brother know. June was amused by all these antics, but later, she was a little ashamed.

In the bleak desolation of the cave and its surroundings, images from her past floated before her eyes, tinged with unreality. Had those events really occurred or was she travelling through a surreal dream?

Her days in the little hill town had soon come to an end.

The elder brother had gone off for higher studies. One after the other, the girls graduated from the local college and went off to the capital city for higher studies too. No, not only studies, June remembered, they went more in search of a better life.

The young man, Joy, had also left after completing his technical course. She didn't distinctly remember when that was and she had lost contact with him. Occasionally, she heard snatches of unconfirmed news about him and that was it.

She didn't continue her studies after graduation but took the teaching job in the little oil town in the northeast.

15

THOUGH SHE WAS happy working in her school, mentally and emotionally June was passing through a disturbing phase at that time—when Joy reappeared in her life.

The only family she had left was that of her father's younger brother. They lived in the village. She had very little contact with them and hardly knew her rapidly growing brood of cousins. After her father's untimely death, she grew up in the house where she had stayed with her mother. She didn't have an unhappy childhood there, with her mother to care for her and her cousins to play with. Though they were poor, they never went hungry. She had started going to school there. At that time she was not old enough to realize what sadness and suffering meant.

She remembered how her mother used to work from morning till night doing various household chores and how she would see her mother silently cry sometimes. When she asked why she was crying, all her mother would say was, 'I'm thinking about your father—I miss him.'

June tried to recall her mother's illness. She could not remember any doctor coming to see her. *Did my mother die without any treatment?* She fell ill one day and died within a week. She probably sensed that she was going to die, so she sent a message to her dear cousin. But when she arrived, her mother was not in a state to even speak. She gestured towards June with her eyes and her cousin picked up the hint. Yes, her mother wanted her cousin to take care of June after her death. So when the funeral and rituals were over, she took June with her to the little hill town.

She had no memory of her father, who died when she was a baby. Even the memory of her mother faded with time. She couldn't remember her face clearly any more. A formless blank occupied the space of her mother's face in her memory. Instead, she constructed a picture of her mother from what she heard from her aunt. It was mostly her imagination; but her imagined picture was the reality for her, the real memory.

After her uncle had retired, his financial condition declined. The number of guests also dwindled. At the same time, the hill people started a long agitation on various issues. The little town also erupted, the local hill people became agitated and the people from the plains who went there for jobs or a livelihood became the target of their dissatisfaction and unreasonable hatred. Random clashes, beatings, house-burning and other violent incidents disturbed the peace of the town.

Then the cowshed of one of their neighbours was burned down by the agitationists. The haystack nearby was also torched. Both burst into flames, which rose very high, lighting the dark early morning sky. In the morning, three cows in the shed were found completely burnt, the charred carcasses lying amongst the ashes, their burned legs twisted grotesquely.

The family left the town immediately after that. And her uncle also moved within a few months.

Despite the wishes of his daughters, June's uncle refused to move to a rented house in Guwahati city since he knew no one there. He decided to settle in his own village, which was starting to grow into a tiny town. His brothers lived there with their families, and other relatives were there too. There were ancestral paddy fields, rice in the family granaries and he knew his retired life would be pleasant in his birthplace.

By that time, all the children had moved away and settled elsewhere.

After two years or so, Joy found her in the small oil town, after searching for her whereabouts.

June was overjoyed to see him, happy to see a known face. Her contact with her cousins had become quite infrequent by then, although the advent of the cell phone allowed a semblance of contact through calls and messages.

Her aunt had become quite dispirited after moving to her husband's ancestral house. June tried to bring her aunt to her town several times to stay with her but she had repeatedly refused. She also went to visit her aunt several times, but her experience was not pleasant. In the large house inhabited by the joint family of her uncle, there flowed a constant current of unspoken tension. The brothers probably never imagined that her uncle would return to settle in the old home or that he was not as well-to-do as they thought he was. There may have been conflict about property too.

But a visit to her own village was always a pleasant experience. She always loved to visit her own village home. Everybody was so pleased with the simple presents she took for them and showed her immense affection. Her father's brothers had even given her a plot of land in the ancestral compound. 'Now that you are working, build a concrete house for yourself here,' they had said.

She was so touched by the gesture that she became nearly speechless. Just the thought of a plot of land, an address, a piece of earth that she could call her own, thrilled her. With the help of her cousins, she had planted few fruit tree saplings in that small plot surrounded by a neatly erected bamboo fence. But then she had thought, *I should give this plot to my eldest uncle's simple-minded daughter. It will help her to get married. Otherwise it will be difficult to get a husband for her.*

So she went back to her school. When Joy told her that he had come to the small oil town for some work and would be staying there a couple of months, June was happy that she would have someone whom she could relate to. Their friendship blossomed. But after Joy left, she seldom met him after that. He said he had to travel a lot to work on his oil project and June had believed every word he said, so smooth were his explanations.

Joy had asked her to help him to obtain cell phone connections. She had a permanent address, all the right documents, so he had three connections from three different mobile companies in her name. That had happened in the early days soon after his arrival in the small town. She didn't know so many connections had been taken by him and had totally forgotten about it.

Suddenly violent incidents started happening all around the town—kidnappings, killings, bank robberies, encounters. The police and the armed forces started combing the small town and its surroundings.

During this time, there was no news of Joy. His cell phone was always switched off. It was then that June suddenly had a premonition, a suspicion that he was up to no good.

And then the news came. Joy sent a boy to meet her with the urgent message that she should immediately get away from the town. The police had recovered the sim cards that were in her name and was already looking for her—she would be arrested soon and booked under the anti-terrorist act, the Terrorist and Disruptive Activities (Prevention) Act (TADA). She had to escape immediately.

The boy said. 'You should move out for some days till the situation cools down.' Joy had made all the arrangements for her—but there was no explanation about the sim cards.

June became totally disoriented at this sudden turn of events. She was frightened to her core and totally stunned by Joy's betrayal. She left the town in a terror-filled daze, escorted by the boy who led her to a safe house some distance away. And that is how her uncertain underground life started in the numerous safe houses arranged by Joy—as, against her conscious will, she sank deeper into a life not of her choosing.

The headlines on newspapers screamed: 'Top underground female insurgent escapes the police dragnet...', her photograph gazing out of front pages.

Against her volition, full of fear and incomprehension, she had to travel from shelter to shelter. Dragged into the circle of underground politics, she ultimately drifted into the mountain camp and then the cave. She had met Joy once or twice in that underground life but never alone, always in a group. They didn't talk—she was surprised at her robot-like state of mind, almost like a zombie. She felt that the poisonous boil which festered within her could not burst and drain out, but froze and shrank into a hard tumour that remained within her. Years passed by. She tried to remember his face, but her memory failed her. Everything had become a blur—his face, his voice, his mannerisms.

In the camp she heard snatches of information about him, nothing concrete, more in the nature of gossip but intriguing nonetheless. She heard he had changed camp; had surrendered, had become a police informer, had gone into business with some surrendered militants. She heard all that news about his new avatar, but felt nothing. Nothing touched her any more. She had remained totally indifferent to the goings-on around her.

If her leaders now ordered her to shoot Joy, would she be able to do it? Would she? Yes, perhaps she would, mechanically, disinterestedly. She had shot a man before. It had happened during an encounter about two years back. On a misty morning, a fierce encounter had suddenly broken out with the armed forces, gunshots blasting the quiet and plumes of smoke thickening the air. She was lying on the ground with her rifle propped on a boulder when she saw a man appear menacingly through the mist and smoke. She had raised her gun and pulled the trigger—then saw the man fall.

She had no reaction to the incident except total indifference. She only thought once or twice about whether the man had fallen to her bullet or was hit by someone else's. Bullets had flown like hailstones during that encounter.

Now, if ordered, she would be able to shoot Joy. And to her utter horror, she knew she could do it emotionlessly, coldly, like swatting a mosquito. She could kill him without rancour, without hatred.

A cold shiver ran through her body with this realization....

16

AFTER A FEW DAYS in the cave, June caught herself thinking bitterly, *What does he think of himself? Considers himself a big leader who can order everyone around! He behaves as if I am his slave. I will show Ron some day who I really am.* Bitter gall rose to her mouth.

June didn't like the way she was thinking. *It is this accursed cave, this bleak mountain landscape, the drudgery of daily thankless chores inside that is making me bitter. These are shrinking me, yes, shrinking me, as a person, as a woman.*

On the very first night in the cave those who didn't have sentry duty immediately fell asleep. The leader also slept early in the centre of the cave where his stretcher was placed. Only Ron and June were awake. Ron shone the beam of his torch into every nook and cranny of the cave, systematically examining it from end to end. He took stock of the food store inside the cave, trying to work out a mental picture as to how he would arrange and distribute it. The small fire built near the leader's stretcher threw dancing shadows of Ron's silhouette on the cave walls. From the other side of the stretcher and the fire, June watched Ron and his shadow. She had sat slumped against the opposite wall since the evening.

She could make out that Ron also looked at her from the dark corners of the cave from time to time. The movement of his shadow would stop momentarily when he looked at her. *He must have seen my eyes glowing like a cat's in the darkness*, June thought.

He had not said anything, neither had she.

Ron had slowly moved away to the other end of the cave, where there was a passage leading outside. June sat there like a statue, clutching her knees to her chest for a long time. Disjointed thoughts passed through her mind like floating clouds in a dry blue sky!

Once she had reached the cave underneath the lonely mountain range, she felt that her past was rapidly slipping away from her memory. Though most of the time she had only ruminated on her past, she felt the memories becoming hazier. Her mind was becoming blank like a white sheet.

After roaming through the mountains for so many days, the cave felt comforting. And they had food now, quite a lot of it—rice, pulses, oil, milk powder, even dry shrunken potatoes that looked like large stones. Nearly everything, except fresh greens!

When the food store was first checked, the leader had become quite voluble. He practically gloated, 'Ah, I should have brought a good stock of dried mithun meat and dried fish too. That's what I overlooked. The whole cave is like a refrigerator. Things don't go bad here.'

Somehow his boasting jarred June's sensibilities. But the next day, the leader had declared her to be the in-charge of the food stores, the quarter master.

Pradip, who had looked after food rationing during the journey, had joked, 'You are the quartermaster of a well-stocked store. I was the quartermaster of only hunger.'

Everybody laughed and agreed that there could be no better quartermaster than her, but she suddenly thought she had been assigned the job only because she was a woman—a gender-determined role!

She was not surprised. In an unspoken way, it was clear that she had to take care of the cooking too. Everyone helped—a system was devised by which everyone who was free helped her to cook and wash the dishes and rudimentary plastic plates afterwards.

She would mostly stay near the fireplace and her battered cooking pots. In the lazy and boring afternoons when the cave was at its quietest, most of the boys went out to do chores and the leader, exhausted by his morning talking, bathing and physiotherapy sessions, would be sleeping. June would sit there near the kitchen, mostly without eating her portion of lunch, and would think disjointed thoughts.

She remembered the second cousins she grew up with in the small hill town. They were never tired of speaking out about women's rights at every opportunity. It was from them that she learned how men would push women to carry out certain roles determined by gender in a male-dominated world. That's how men always try to dominate and subjugate women, but those beliefs didn't prevent the girls from catching hold of rich men to make use of.

I shouldn't be so uncharitable towards them, June silently chided herself. *They have always showed friendship and affection towards me. The small tiffs we had were really too insignificant.* Till the mobile sim cards thrust her into this underground life, she had had regular and pleasant contact with them, though not very frequently.

June felt a shiver coursing through her body in the warm comfortable nook of the cave.

How many days had passed in this cave? Quite some days now. She tried to remember but got confused. Then she suddenly realized that nobody seemed to be discussing going out from the cave! They must be planning a long rest, each and every one of them, more interested in organizing a mini camp in the cave.

The leader had forcefully said that everyone must follow strict military discipline in the cave just like they had done in the main camp.

Nobody said anything. Ron only nodded.

'Don't forget,' the leader had stressed. 'Though we are relatively safe in this cave for the time being, we are still in the midst of a war. We can never let our guard down, even for a moment. To emerge victorious in the future, we must get out of this situation alive.'

Spoken like a real leader, June had thought. But then she observed everyone. All were silent, their faces expressionless. They were not taken in by the leader's words—even Ron was silent.

Then suddenly, Ron yelled a belated three cheers. June observed that the other boys took up the cheer loudly and clearly, the cave reverberating with their shouts.

The leader smiled contentedly.

Then he had formally declared Ron as the commander of the cave camp. Pradip had become his deputy. She was already the store in-charge, the quartermaster. Not only that—she was the cook, nurse, attendant all rolled into one. That left the others as rank-and-file, the foot soldiers.

She had been doing her assigned job perfectly. Cooking, cleaning and nursing the paralysed leader. During that time, when she cleaned, bathed, fed the leader like a professional nurse, she always had a smile on her face. She observed that while she was cleaning and bathing the leader, he would always keep his eyes tightly shut, faint lines creasing his forehead, indicating his inner turmoil at his helplessness. She could make out his genuine gratitude at her ministrations, yes, she could feel it. He had called her 'daughter' several times and even had jokingly said, 'If I had married early as the boys used to do in our village, I would by now have a daughter your age.'

She remembered she had smiled sweetly at his words, but they had failed to touch any inner chord. Later she thought, *Why am I becoming like this ? So indifferent, so insensitive, as if my feelings are blunted. They think they are keeping me safe by ensuring I stay inside the cave. They do not realize how suffocating it is, how restless I am feeling, how small parts of me are dying every day. They have tried to show consideration for me, they have made arrangements for my privacy, for my comfort, but I don't want this. I want to go out, stand on sentry duty, doing other outside chores like the boys, and that's what exactly I am going to do. I'll go out right now to bring firewood, leaves, grass, like the others.*

At that moment, Ron had come in and began giving her instructions. She didn't reply, but turned her face away and then moved away in a huff.

Ron was surprised by her behaviour. He came closer and asked her softly, 'What's the matter, June, are you feeling all right?'

Even then she didn't reply, but went out from the cave. After a while, she could sense that Ron had come out of the cave. She suddenly turned back to face him. He stopped.

To her surprise, June found herself speaking to Ron in an excited tone, 'I will not always stay confined to the cave. It's suffocating—and I will die here, surely I will. I want to go out, do all the chores outside, do sentry duty, everything. I will not remain confined to this hole.'

Ron was taken aback by her controlled outburst. He became silent. She didn't look at him any more, but gazed at the mountains which created a dark silhouette against a luminous indigo sky where large stars shone in clusters.

She saw a bank of mist rolling in from the valleys like a moving wall. There was a chilly bite in the air that was refreshing after the stale air inside the cave.

She heard Ron saying softly, 'Okay, we will see that you have a change.'

17

FROM WHERE SHE stood near the stony ledge outside the cave, June had a panoramic view of the snow-capped mountains in front. With the first shafts of the morning sun striking the mountains, they rapidly changed colour, sometimes becoming so clear that the ridges, crevices and other details were etched sharply against the sky.

On a brilliant sunny day, they would appear to be very near, close enough to be touched.

June thought, *What a marvellous scene! So beautiful, yet at the same time frightening too. In front of such majestic magnificence, small people like us can't but feel how insignificant we are.*

June didn't notice Ron coming outside, but when she saw him standing next to her, she didn't say anything. She had barely uttered two words to him the last few days. It was not that she had talked much before, but they had been civil with each other and she had told him about some snippets from her past.

Now, she was perplexed at her own behaviour—was it some kind of protest? She couldn't figure it out and that made her angry with herself.

Ron, however, began talking.

'Look at the snowline—snow is streaming through some crevices. The wind-blown slopes have hardly any snow, but the other ones are gleaming white. Look at the blue-green area below the snowline, the craggy mountain face, the jutting rocks and the deep shadowed gullies. See, see, the deep gullies are covered with heavy forests…'

It was as if he was talking to himself and she was merely a sounding board.

'Look at those narrow valleys between the ridges. They are covered by dense forests and go down gradually one after the other like steps. The creek near our cave is luxuriantly green where a dense clump of pines has grown.'

June was forced to look down into the valleys though she didn't want to. Ron went on.

'Most of the time, the valleys are covered with a dense canopy of mist; only the tops of the tall trees float above it. Today everything is crystal clear. We can see everything very clearly.'

June had observed that Ron would keenly scan the mountains and the valleys below for a long time with his pair of bulky binoculars. Where was it? In the cave or his heavy haversack?

'Through each valley flows a gurgling stream of clear water. In the bigger valleys, there may be as large or small rivers. These drain the snow melt from the mountains and join each other to form the big rivers in our place—Assam.'

Ron was silent for some time. Yet she waited eagerly in anticipation of his next words. June had thought that he was looking for a way for them to go down, But no, he was observing the 'primeval and virgin forests' about which he waxed so eloquently.

'I want to go down to explore the valleys below,' Ron suddenly said. June turned towards him sharply. His eyes were shining, The brown eyes, with their black pupils, were shining unnaturally. He looked towards June and their eyes met. He observed the amazement and a shadow of fear in her eyes.

'I want to go down within two or three days,' Ron said. 'I will take someone with me'

June wanted to say, 'I will go with you', but suppressed the urge at the last moment, thinking she would not be allowed to. Neither Ron nor the leader would allow it. She could feel that the leader had become extremely possessive about her. Whenever she went out he would look solemn and when she returned, he would closely scrutinize her. If he felt she had a good time outside, he would behave like a jealous child and tell her depressing and frightening stories about the potential dangers there. And when he felt that she had returned depressed he would try to joke with her to make her smile. It had become a pattern, predictable and boring.

Pradip joined them at that moment. He had heard the last part of Ron's words. June saw that Pradip's eyes were glistening. It was clear that Pradip really wanted to go down with Ron, but he also realized that he couldn't do so. He was second in command and had to remain with the leader.

'Yes, we should think about food. The stores in the cave have to be replenished,' Pradip said.

Ron nodded. 'Any addition would be surely welcome. We may have to stay in the cave for some time,' he added.

'Yes, the helicopters are still on search missions. Only yesterday, a pair of them flew by—at a great distance, of course.'

'It may be a routine sortie. Yes, they may still be looking for our boys. And they will do so for some time—at least to prevent us from regrouping.'

'Yes, they want us on the run.'

'That's only natural. We are actually on the run, aren't we?' Pradip laughed hollowly.

'We have some time, but one day we will have to make the move. The leader said the best time would be in early winter, before or after the first snowfall. I agree with him. That will be the best time. With the onset of winter, the enemy's guard will also lessen.'

'That's for sure—they will be less vigilant then.'

'Yeah, that's the plan, but we will have to go down from the winter snowline before the start of heavy snowfall. All these areas will be under several feet of snow then and difficult to cross.'

June had a feeling that what was left unsaid was the condition of the leader. Though he had carried on with great fortitude, there was no real improvement. He couldn't move his legs, though occasionally, spasmodic movements would occur. Though he could move the arms a little he couldn't lift them properly. The muscles in his limbs were shrinking and becoming leaner. To June it looked as if his muscles were melting internally.

She had told Ron about it.

'Disuse atrophy,' he had promptly replied.

The next day, he examined the limbs of the leader himself. June thought Ron looked like a real doctor with his grave expression and methodical examination.

'We shall have to start more active and vigorous physiotherapy,' he had announced.

The leader seemed very pleased. He profusely thanked Ron.

Active physiotherapy was soon started. Ron had deputed two boys to take turns in massaging and moving the limbs in all the joints twice daily, morning and evening.

During and after the sessions the leader would be in high spirits. He would talk happily with the boys and would thank them profusely after the sessions ended. From time to time, Ron would personally supervise the sessions.

After some days, June had to admit that Ron's physiotherapy was not without results. Though there was no marked improvement it looked as if the deterioration had been stopped somehow.

It was after one such session, when the leader was in a very good mood, that Ron broached the subject of going down.

June remembered that the leader's face clouded a little. She could feel he was more afraid than angry. His insecurity showed clearly in his face, but Ron was not looking at him. Then the leader put on a brave face and said, 'Think hard, Ron. Weigh the pros and cons. Would it be advisable to expose oneself to unnecessary dangers?'

'It's a risk worth taking, sir,' Ron had replied.

'Do you really hope to find any food there?'

'Unlikely, but you never know.'

'As far as I remember, there are no human habitations nearby,' the leader said.

'Even if there are, we should not attempt to make contact with them. It's too dangerous now.'

'You are right,' the leader readily agreed.

'You have stocked enough food here to last us through the winter, if required. The boys have also collected a sizable stockpile of woods and twigs for fuel. Still, if we can add to the stock, no harm in it,' Ron said.

June remembered that someone had pointed to the mushrooms that grew in the rocky meadows and under the conifers. The moment the leader had heard about the mushrooms, he expressly forbade them to even think about it.

'Those are almost always poisonous,' he had said, 'a small piece is capable of killing a man. Even the local experts find it difficult to make out which mushroom is poisonous and which one is not. I have seen the tragedy of eating poisonous mushrooms—once a whole family died within hours as blood poured out of all the pores of the body. Mushrooms are out.'

That scared them so much that there was no further talk of gathering mushrooms for food.

One day, June did not get involved with the cooking as she normally did. She ignored the boy who came to help her to cook. After some time, she rose from the spot near the fireplace where she was sitting, went to her sleeping place in the corner of the cave and, turning her back to the fireplace, lay down to sleep.

The leader saw her, so did Ron. No one said anything. Ron started cooking with the boy whose turn it was to help that day.

June was seething with anger. Why did no one understand her, what she liked, what her needs were? They thought they were protecting her, trying to make her comfortable in every way, had even built her a secluded corner to sleep inside the cave, created partitions with sacks of stored food and wooden planks, made her an exclusive toilet… but they didn't understand her real needs.

I will not stay inside the cave like a rat, she thought bitterly, even if they wanted her too. *If they order me to stay inside the cave, I will not do so. I will not obey such an order. There is nobody around this godforsaken place. There are no enemies close by, no such danger. Then why shouldn't I go out? Tomorrow I will go out for a long, long time.*

The next morning when she got up, she behaved as if nothing had happened the day before. She could see the unhappy, drawn face of the leader, but she ignored it. She cooked the morning meal and completed her chores. Then she silently dressed in her camp uniform, put on her battered boots and got ready for her adventure.

The leader was silently watching her but didn't say anything. Ron was not inside the cave. June had seen him going out in the morning with his binoculars.

She fed the leader like she used to do every day. Then

she casually said. 'I will go out for a long time today. I really feel suffocated staying inside the cave.'

The leader didn't say anything. June realized how helpless he was. She stopped, sat near him and said in a cheerful voice. 'The weather is very pleasant today. The sun is soft and warming. I don't know where Ron and the others have gone. I feel they must take you out in weather like this. At least to the forest, if it's not too far!' She somehow felt good after saying that. 'I have told Ron several times,' she added.

She saw the eyes of the leader brighten.

'I also want to go outside,' he said. 'To constantly remain in a supine position like this, is suffocating. In that explosion, my brain should have been destroyed or I should have died. Now see my condition—an active brain and mind imprisoned in a useless body. Can there be a greater curse than this?'

June suddenly felt worried.

'There is also another consideration,' the leader went on, 'it is not easy to carry me out. That drop beyond the ledge is about ten feet. It will take four men to carry me down and up, not easy at all. That's why I have not requested a trip out.'

'Ron should have asked you.'

The leader laughed dryly. Then he said, 'I know you are bored staying inside the cave. You go out. Have a good and vigorous walk around. That will do you good, but don't go far. The forest would be quite far. Go up to the sentry posts, but come back soon. I don't like staying alone in the cave.'

'I won't go before Ron returns. He will stay with you when I go out.'

'Okay, okay, good enough,' the leader sounded relieved. He started to talk to June about the food stock in their store and June understood that he felt much better after reviewing the food situation with her. She also felt good.

As soon as Ron came back, she stood up. The leader said, 'I have allowed her to go and spend some time outside.' Then in a lighter vein he added, 'Otherwise she will grumble at all of us if she stays inside the cave.'

Ron didn't say anything.

June slowly come out of the cave without looking at anyone or saying anything.

'Oh!' the bright light outside nearly blinded her. It wasn't that she had not come out beyond the ledge before. She had been out of the cave quite often, from the front as well as the down-sloping back side where a narrow passage opened up in another mountain face and gradually went down to a gully. In an offshoot of the way down, the boys had built a small secluded toilet and bathroom for her with tree branches. It was an unthinkable luxury for her and she was ever grateful to Ron for that.

She met Pradip and another boy outside. They had huge loads of firewood on their backs which they carried with a head-sling, hill people style.

'Aha, in full dress!' Pradip said. 'Where are you going?'

'Today I have been given time off to stay outside for a couple of hours.'

'To stay outside?' Pradip asked incredulously, 'Given leave to wander on your own?'

'Yes, you all roam outside practically the whole day, while I stay in that dark cave. It's too claustrophobic. Moreover, all the vitamins in my body will disappear.'

'Vitamins disappear?' Pradip sounded shocked. He quickly put down his bundle of firewood below the cave ledge and returned. 'What vitamin will disappear and how?'

'Women who are constantly kept inside the house become sickly. I will also suffer the same fate. Ah, what vitamin was that? Yes, vitamin D, which the sunlight gives.'

Both of them laughed loudly.

'Okay, then sit in the sun on this rock. I will go to the cave and eat. I am famished'

'Yes, go. Ron could not have eaten either—ladle his food out for him,' June said.

18

JUNE SAT ON a boulder in the afternoon sun. She could feel a refreshing nip in the air—but still, coming out of the cave and sitting in the afternoon sun didn't lift her spirits.

She felt both lonely and depressed.

What would she do now? All alone in this mountainous meadow? If only someone would take her out on a march! While they were in the camp, they used to go out for long marches. Sometimes the boys and girls would go together but usually it was the women who would frequently march out. They would take the long road to the villages and would came back to the camp after an hour or two, drenched with sweat. They would often go out without any arms, but sometimes they took their guns with them and carried backpacks on their shoulders.

They also sang during the marches. She tried to remember the songs, but couldn't

She saw Pradip hurriedly coming out from the cave. He came straight to her.

'Have you eaten? June asked.

He nodded

'And did you give Ron some food?'

'Yes.' Then he said, 'Come, let's go!'

'Go? Where?' June was genuinely surprised.

'Why, let's move around. Go out for a walk.'

'You must have told the leader and Ron that I am sitting all alone on a stone outside, and they must have told you to take me out a little since I must be feeling low. Isn't that so?'

Pradip's sheepish smile said it all. He said, 'Come now, let's go—get up from that stone.'

'If you have been assigned the duty to take me out, then let's go. I don't want you to fail in your duties.' June got up from the stone, smiling. Suddenly she felt better, much better. Her feeling of loneliness also disappeared. She felt like talking.

'Cooking the same stuff every day is getting on my nerves,' she said to Pradip. 'The potatoes have all shrunk and their taste has also changed. They have become hard and sweet. They must have been in the cave for quite a long time.'

'Couldn't be very old.'

'How can you say that?'

'About three months ago, we bought lots of potatoes from local farmers.'

'I didn't see any potato sellers in the camp.'

'They don't come to the camp. Agents buy them from the producers for us. We build up a stock in the village and when it's sufficient, we transport it to the camps. A part of that stock may have found its way to this cave also.'

'All potatoes that are stored in the mountains must be turning hard and sweet. There must be some other way of cooking them.'

'I have seen one thing,' Pradip said. 'The mountain folk boil the potatoes for a long time, keeping them in an earthen pitcher with hot water near the fireplace. Then they mash it for a long time to make a fine mixture. Probably that's the way to eat shrunken potatoes.'

'Maybe,' June replied.

'Is the leader eating properly?' Pradip asked.

'You can't say he does. In the morning I usually give him rice and lentils cooked together. He eats that, but after a few days he usually asks me not to give him any more. I try to cook a good meal for him, but he doesn't eat much. He likes chocolates, but we have so few—he doesn't complain though.'

'And what about Ron sir?'

'Don't ask me. He is like a monk. He doesn't pay any attention to what he eats.'

They remained silent for some time. They had crossed the stony outcroppings and were about to reach an area densely covered with bushes and thickets. Pradip said, 'There is a sentry post ahead. Today's password is "Poisonous snake".'

'"Poisonous snake"!' June laughed on hearing the password.

When they reached the post Kumbang, who was on sentry duty, barked 'Halt! What's the password?' He was smiling.

June and Pradip immediately responded in unison, 'Poisonous snake!'

All of them laughed.

The inside of the sentry post, carefully designed by Ron, was quite spacious, more like a pillbox. With the bottom dug in, it had a roof of thick branches. Stones were piled atop and around like a wall. All three of them could enter it easily.

'The sentry post is quite comfortable,' June said.

'Only one problem,' Kumbang said. 'If I see something suspicious while I am on duty here, there is no way to communicate with the cave. Sentries don't have permission to leave the post,' he said.

Pradip looked around and thought, *Has Ron sir overlooked this aspect? I shall have to bring it to his notice.*

'When are we planning to leave this place?' Kumbang suddenly blurted out. Then he hesitated, his face flushed red. In his nervousness he stuck out his tongue and bit it.

June and Pradip remained silent for some time.

'The final decision will be taken by our leaders,' Pradip started slowly. 'They have said that we shall have to move as soon as snow falls, but before it gets heavy. How do you like it here? I like this place very much. The cave and the dry grass beds are comfortable.'

'I wonder where Ron sir has learned to make beds with dry grass. The first layer is grass with soil below—they are called clods. You put them on the cave floor and beat them into a flat surface, with the grass side up. Over that is a layer of grass so that the cold from the cave floor cannot seep in from below.'

'The layers get more than six inches thick, like a real mattress. When I first gathered the long grass, I had no idea how it would be used,' Pradip said.

'I put two blankets over the grass for the leader. Over that I have placed a sheet. It's like a proper hospital bed, which he needs,' June concluded.

'It is becoming colder day by day. We will need more blankets,' Kumbang said. 'I feel very cold at night. So I always sleep with Pradip, never alone.'

'There are a few more blankets in the cave,' June said, 'still in their cellophane wrappings. If the cold increases, we have to get them out. But the cave is quite warm, isn't it?'

'You sleep quite near the fire so you feel warm. Late at night, the cave really becomes cold. Where we sleep, it's quite cold. And the place where Ron sir sleeps, near the entrance, is the coldest.'

'I kept an extra blanket in his bed, but he didn't take it. He picked it up, folded it and kept it back in the store. He is becoming more and more like a monk.'

They remained silent for some time.

'Now he is talking about going down to explore the valley below,' June said.

'Who? Who is talking of going down?' Kumbang asked.

'Who else but Monk sir. He will take one of the boys with him.'

'Monk sir, Monk sir!' everyone laughed uproariously inside the dug-out sentry post, feeling lighthearted. They talked freely.

'Monk sir pays no attention to what he eats, what he wears, how he lives. He is indifferent to everything. He's always deep in some thought, but I don't know what he thinks about. To me he appears to be meditating.'

'I have also observed that.'

'Have you? It is not that he has started brooding only after coming here. Even in the camp, he was silent and thoughtful.'

'He was not like this before. I have known him for many years. He was a totally different person in the past.'

June and Pradip looked at Kumbang in surprise. Kumbang was very young, he looked barely twenty years old.

'Long back? Where did you see him?' June and Pradip asked together.

'In our village. He used to stay in a house near ours.'

'Where?'

'Where? In our village.'

'Your village? Where is your village?'

'Our village? Our village is in Assam. On the northern bank of the Brahmaputra, near a river.'

'Oh!' Pradip sounded exasperated. 'Don't talk in a roundabout way.'

Kumbang smiled. June observed that when he smiled, Kumbang looked very beautiful.

'A big river flows near our village.'

'Kumbang!' Pradip shouted. 'What river? Subansiri?'

'No, no, not that river, but its tributary, the Dikrong.'

'The Dikrong river! Dikrong!' Both of them exclaimed together.

'Yes, I first saw Ron sir there, on the banks of the Dikrong river. I was then a young boy, quite young. I used to wear half pants then.'

'What was Ron sir doing there?'

'He was working there.'

June and Pradip looked at each other. Kumbang went on slowly, 'He was quite slim then, slim and tall. His eyes always shone with urgency—urgency and impatience.'

June wondered what work Ron was doing on the banks of the Dikrong. 'Tell us, Kumbang, tell us about it, tell us the whole story,' she pleaded.

19

THE DAY WAS very cold, the sky dull grey. It was dim in the cave even at noon. A light breeze brought in the mountain cold into the cave.

The leader was in his bed. Ron had made him a recliner where he could be propped up a little. It was rudimentary but the leader was very happy with it. It gave him a more commanding position than the flat bed. Ron was tending the fire, trying to stoke a nearly smokeless fire.

The leader, reclining with a monkey cap placed on his head and covered by a blanket, moved a little and said, 'I know how to make wood charcoal, but it would be very difficult to make it here. Smoke would be the main problem since it'll signal our presence. Yesterday, as you know, a helicopter flew quite nearby.'

Ron sat near the leader, who looked out at the mountains visible from the cave mouth. A grey swirling mist slowly rose from the forest below and soon shrouded the mountains.

'Ron,' the leader started hesitantly. 'When we go from here…' His voice trailed off.

'Yes, sir,' Ron leaned forward to catch his words.

'Hold my hand, Ron.'

Ron placed his hand over the leader's, noticing how dry and cold his skin felt.

'When we go from here,' the leader started again. 'I want you to do me a favour.'

'Yes, sir.'

'Take me home. I want to stay at home for the rest of my days.'

Ron was about to say some consoling or encouraging words like he always did. But the leader cut him short with an emphatic nod. Then indicating his limbs with his eyes, he said, 'These have become useless. I don't think I will be able to walk again. I have decided to retire from the organization—and after this decision I am at peace with myself. Totally at peace.' The leader sounded really pleased.

'Yes, sir,' Ron said a little uncertainly, not knowing how to respond to this new request.

The leader went on, 'Yes, Ron, when we leave this cave, I would like you to take me to my home. My home is in a village on the bank of a very large river, the Subansiri. My father stays there along with my unmarried elder sister. He is quite old now, but he was going strong when I last saw him. He used to work in the post and telegraph department and after retirement, gets a pension. I think he has been getting his pension for many more years than those spent serving the government.' The leader chuckled.

Not knowing how to respond, Ron just made a guttural sound. The leader continued.

'My mother died long ago. My elder brother also works

in the postal department. He is posted in a far-off place in south India. I have four sisters, two older than me and two younger. Three sisters are married and stay at different places. Only my unmarried sister lives with my father. She is a deaf-mute, you know, since her birth. Give me some water, Ron.'

Ron brought some lukewarm water from the kettle near the fireplace, and held up the glass to the leader's lips. He drank greedily and then asked for more.

When Ron wiped the water that had dribbled over his chin, the leader started again.

'My deaf-mute sister looks after my father, and she does it admirably. She lovingly cooks for my father who unlike me, enjoys a good square meal. In fact, he does not eat anything that has not been cooked or prepared by my sister. He simply won't.'

The leader's voice trailed off and he was lost in a reverie for a long time. Ron waited. After some time the leader started to speak again.

'I know she will look after me well once I am home. There are also other people at home. My mother had given small homestead plots in a corner of our large compound to two families of ploughmen who work for us. The men look after the cultivation of our land and their womenfolk work at our household and keep my sister company. There are half a dozen children between these two families. Our compound is always full of sounds of children playing, their laughter. I would like to be there—amidst that life…'

Ron felt as if the leader was baring his inner self to him.

It was a sort of confession. He felt a little uneasy, a lump in his throat. The leader's hand moved a little under his palm. He couldn't yet raise his hands but was capable of moving them side-to-side on the bed.

He continued, 'My deaf-mute sister would understand my needs perfectly. In fact, she understands everybody's needs. And she loves children. She is like an aunt to most of the village children. She probably knows she will never have children of her own, yet she loves children so much! I sometimes feel God is so unfair.'

Ron was unable to find any words to say. He kept nodding his head and massaging the leader's hand.

'I will be happy there, in my home.'

'Yes, sir, I don't doubt it.'

'An invalid like me will be a liability to everyone here, a liability to the organization.'

'Sir, how about staying in another country? You would be safe there, whereas in Assam, the police and armed forces won't let you be. From another country, you could advise us and guide the movement.'

Ron saw the leader's eyes light up like two light bulbs. Ron felt a tremor passing through his body, but then slowly, his eyes dimmed.

'It is a tempting thought, Ron,' he said slowly. 'Thank you very much. But you don't know many things. I want to be at home, at least for a few months. I am very tired, you know. I have been travelling constantly for the last couple of years; here today, there tomorrow. No, I want to go home.'

'But we need to have a thorough health check-up done. We have to explore all the avenues for your medical treatment. Maybe surgery would work,' Ron said.

'You have a point there, but my own feeling is that nothing much would come out of it.'

'No, no, sir. You cannot say that,' Ron protested.

'Ha ha, Ron. Life and experience have taught me certain things. The worst injury a man can have is a spinal injury and I have exactly that. It has nearly paralysed me from the neck downwards, making me a total invalid.'

This time it was Ron who spoke forcefully.

'The first priority is to get you out of here to Assam and then to any other place where you would be safe. The next thing is your check-up and treatment. All others plans, including going home, come after that. And we will take a decision about what to do only once we reach the plains.'

The leader closed his eyes, as if trying to fight back tears.

'I give you my word, sir,' Ron began cautiously. 'Come what may, I will see that you go home. I will personally take you there.'

'I know you will do that,' the leader said, without opening his eyes. 'I know.'

They remained silent for quite a long time, each immersed in their own thoughts.

Ron felt a chill creeping up his feet. He looked at the fire. The blaze was cheerfully throwing myriad dancing shadows on the cave walls.

The leader opened his eyes, a film of tears blurring

his vision. He looked at the opening of the cave mouth. The swirling mist that had risen from the valley was crowding outside the cave mouth. After some time, he turned his gaze to the fire. Ron was also looking intently into the fire.

'Ron, I want to tell you a story,' the leader said.

'Yes, sir.'

'I will tell you about a case I went to investigate once, Ron.' He was his own self again! Sharp and confident.

Ron wondered why the leader was in a talkative mood today—*did he want to remember the past to forget the present?*

'It was after one of those periodic military operations against us which they give fancy names to—Operation this-or-that. One of our senior regional leaders went missing. You may have known him also. He was an important leader so I was troubled. We could find no trace of him. We thought probably he had been secretly arrested and killed. We could not even declare him a martyr unless his body was found.'

The leader paused for breath.

Unseen by the leader, Ron closed his eyes for a second. The story sounded very familiar! If someone went missing, they had to search for him. If he died, they would declare him a martyr to the cause. If alive, they had to investigate, to find out whether he had turned traitor. In that case they had to kill him, summarily carrying out revolutionary justice. Ron breathed in the stale air of the cave....

'It was then that he surfaced,' the leader declared dramatically.

'Sir?' Ron came out of his reverie.

'His family had a "pam" at one of those large riverine islands of the Brahmaputra. A very secluded and obscure place that has no regular communications, a place totally cut off from the outside world. You have to cross several small channels to reach it. The main occupation of the villagers was rearing buffalo herds, what we call "moh khuti". We got to know that our leader was staying there and had started farming.'

Ron could picture the lonely, desolate landscape—he had seen many such places, typically covered with tall seasonal grass, scarce stunted trees, rich silt soil suitable for winter crops of potatoes, mustard and vegetables. The sky above, blue and vast, sometimes seemed to close in, like a suffocating dome. The stillness, the loneliness, emphasized the unreal aura that pervaded these villages.

'He was farming there,' the leader went on, 'and accompanying him was one of our other boys, a dim-witted fellow with a single eye. We didn't know what to do with that idiot really. And there was another specimen with him, an old Nepali who had left his home and had forgotten where it was. He would sit hunched up the whole day with a straw hat on his head and tend the vegetable patch, which was really luxuriant when I went there. Are you listening to me, Ron?'

'Yes, sir, I was thinking that I have seen such places.'

'They are not uncommon in those char areas.'

'Yes, sir, then what happened?'

'We reached there at mid-morning. He was not at

home, but the Nepali was there. Our boys found the other two working in the fields some way off, tending rows of potato plants. The boys, as usual in such situations, surrounded them and marched them to the hut where I was sitting.'

Ron could imagine the scene: bringing in the fugitives under guard, followed by a harsh questioning session, conducted as a sort of kangaroo court. Sometimes this resulted in a summary execution… Ron felt a sickness in the pit of his stomach, not wanting to hear any more. He wanted to scream…

'And do you know what I saw?' the leader asked. 'I faced a totally defeated man, a man utterly demolished, broken down. It didn't matter to him any more whether he lived or died. The spark of life seemed to have died within him. I never expected that. The man was good as dead.'

Yes, the man of the past had died, thought Ron, *but perhaps a new man was reborn with the growth of his planted crops. As the seeds germinate and leaves unfold, as plants grow and mist rises from the river and marshes, with the bright moonlight casting shadows in the ground, with the cooing of the morning doves, a new man was being reborn?*

'What did you do, sir?' Ron gulped as he asked.

'I took one last hard look at him, at the one-eyed dimwit and the old Nepali who had forgotten where his home was and felt a shiver running through my whole body and soul.'

'Sir?' Ron became fully attentive.

'I ordered our local unit to leave them alone, never to disturb them again. In fact, never to set foot on that char again as I felt it was an afflicted place with an evil presence. Then I gave both of them their discharge from the organization in writing and left the place as fast as I could. It is impossible to face such a defeated man for long. Impossible.'

20

THE NEXT DAY, when Ron went out with Kumbang to explore the valley below, the leader became very despondent and irritable. He complained to June, 'Why did he have to go down to the valley? What will he find there? Even if he finds some game, say a deer, he won't be able to kill it. I have strictly forbidden shooting. At the most he can clobber some frogs.'

Then, warming up to the subject of frog-eating, the leader said, 'The mountain valley frogs can be very tasty, you know? After cooking them, you will not be able to make out the difference from a cooked chicken.' Then his tone changed again, 'I wish we had a powerful crossbow. I could have made one. I know how to make it, but now with these useless hands…'

June noted the desperation in his voice and his eyes glistening with unshed tears. She anxiously asked herself, *Am I imagining things?*

The leader went on and on, trying to establish to June how useless Ron's expedition was likely to be. 'A sheer wastage of time and effort,' he said. 'Sheer wastage, a useless expedition and dangerous too….'

However, in Ron's absence, he also became quite active. June thought he was a little frightened too. He asked all the boys to stay near the cave. The outside forward sentry posts were brought near the exits of the cave so that he could feel their presence all along, especially at night.

He also made an arrangement where he could be carried in a makeshift stretcher to the ledge outside the cave mouth where the sunshine fell in abundance. He would have his head covered with an old umbrella that was found inside the cave and sun himself for a long time in the winter morning sun. During that time, he would talk with Pradip or one of the boys who was with him. He would then take a long nap in the sun.

It will only do him good, thought June. *The sun warming his limbs and weak muscles may really help him to recover.*

During those sunning sessions, June wouldn't stay with the leader. She would arrange everything and then would come back inside the cave. A patch of sunlight also fell inside the cave mouth for quite some time. June would pull up a wooden block there and sit silently. From that place she and the leader couldn't see each other, but she could hear what the leader and the boys were saying.

From the conversation she heard, she could make out that the leader was trying to get to know the boys as closely as possible. After a day or two she lost interest and stopped paying any attention. She wondered if he would have talked with the boys so searchingly had he been well. *I don't think so*, she thought. Then trying to put away these thoughts, she hummed to herself. After a while, she discovered that she was making up songs and singing them. Meaningless words and ditties! The discovery amazed her. *I am really going mad*, she thought. 'Sheer boredom is turning me into a mad woman,' she mumbled. 'See, now I have also started mumbling.'

One day, from her sunspot inside the cave, June heard the leader speaking to Pradip intimately. She was surprised and intrigued by his tone. She went a little forward and unseen by them, tried to hear what they were saying.

'With Ron gone out, you are the real camp commander now, Pradip,' the leader said.

'Yes, sir,' Pradip replied in the old camp military style, only a little softly.

The leader then went on to give Pradip some advice, tips of survival in a guerilla war, how to preserve oneself and advance in an underground set-up.

Then he reminded Pradip of their past association, about the time when the leader had visited Pradip's house and talked with his mother and other family members about the large trees in their compound at home.

Why is he talking about all this? June wondered. *It must be for a reason.*

Then he started praising Pradip.

'I have no doubt you will advance. Yes, you will go very far, rise up to be an important leader of the organization. Do you know why? Because you are a dependable and practical man like me, not a dreamer or an intellectual, eh? Intellectuals are necessary,' the leader went on. 'But true intellectuals are very rare. Most are just pretenders. With their gloomy silences and smart philosophical statements, they pretend to be different. Pradip, mark my words, the intellectuals are the first ones to betray a movement.'

June was surprised to hear the leader's words. In the camp he had praised no one. He would only grunt then, and that indecipherable grunt had to be accepted as his approval.

June instantly became more alert, thinking that he was indirectly talking about Ron.

The leader then proceeded to swear Pradip to secrecy, invoking some secret code of the organization.

Pradip took the oath after a pause.

'You will report directly to me and me alone, do you understand that?' the leader said. 'It should be totally confidential. You need not even tell the camp commander.' The last was in a hoarse whisper.

'Yes, sir,' Pradip replied.

'Keep an eye on everyone, everyone, do you understand?'

'Yes, sir.'

'We have to be very careful. The way we have been routed! There must surely have been someone who betrayed us, otherwise it wouldn't have been so easy.'

June immediately felt that a spy cell had come into existence among them.

They were the last nine survivors!

21

Kumbang suddenly grasped Ron's hand.

Ron froze immediately like a statue; only his eyes darted around.

They were crossing a sloping alpine, grassy meadow strewn with rocks and dotted with small shrubs bearing purple flowers. In late autumn, patches of it blazed with tiny daisies. Herders often brought cattle, even yaks, here to graze.

It was at the moment they were halfway across the open meadow, walking as fast as they could, that Kumbang had grasped Ron's hand. Both of them instantly squatted on their haunches. Ron observed that Kumbang was intently looking at a particular spot. Amid the small rocks to their left, something seemed to be moving.

It was a furry animal as big as a cat! It looked like a large fat rat, with a furry coat, short legs and a black-tipped tail. It had keen darting eyes.

Ron saw Kumbang taking something out of his bag. It was a sling. Ron remembered how happy Kumbang had been to find a piece of rubber from a tyre in the cave. And before Ron could even blink an eye, Kumbang brought out a smooth pigeon-egg-sized stone and let it fly from his sling. With accurate marksmanship, the stone hit the animal on its head, stunning and immobilizing it. Kumbang practically flew behind the stone, caught the animal and brought it back.

They took shelter behind some rocks and examined it.

'What is this?' Kumbang asked.

'I think it's an Himalayan marmot. It belongs to the rodent family. Their burrows must be there. You should see what deep and branching burrows they have.'

'Shh…' Kumbang hissed.

Ron saw that two other marmots had appeared, possibly coming out to sun themselves. One was older and bigger, the other a young agile one. The old one possibly suspected something was amiss. It raised its head as if trying to detect a smell, while the younger one moved away some distance. Kumbang lifted his sling again and a stone flew from it, hitting the younger one in the back with such force that it was flung a few feet away. Again, Kumbang flew like a bird. The older one sensing danger, squeaked and immediately got into its burrow. The younger one, incapacitated by the hit, also nearly escaped but Kumbang was able to catch hold of it just as it was about to enter the hole. When he brought back the small animal, its short legs were still moving. He swiftly killed it and the one Ron was holding.

'The fur is so soft!'

'It's very valuable too,' Ron said. 'It's really surprising that you could kill two such shy creatures so quickly.'

'Probably they hadn't come across human beings before.

So they were not very careful,' Kumbang said. His face was all aglow with pleasure.

'Let's go back to the cave today,' Ron said. 'Everyone will welcome fresh meat curry today. We are only about two hours from the cave.'

They waited for nearly an hour for more marmots to appear, but none did. They had probably gone deep into their burrows. 'You are a great hunter, Kumbang. I must congratulate you. Killing a marmot is no easy task.'

There was a celebration in the cave and everybody lent a hand in cooking the meal. June brought out a generous portion of onions and dry chillies from her store, while Kumbang and Pradip pelted and gutted the marmots, lovingly cutting up the tender meat. Kumbang cut the guts into foot-long pieces, inverted them inside out and scraped the inner layers carefully after washing them. Then he sliced the guts into small pieces. 'These also make a good dish,' he said.

Soon the cave was filled with the aroma of cooking meat.

'Today,' the leader joked, 'a hunting dog will be able to smell us out from a long, long distance.'

***

The next day, while Ron and Kumbang were going down to the valley, Kumbang suddenly blurted out, 'I have met you before, long ago. I used to wear half pants then.'

Ron was pleasantly startled. 'What? You've met me? When?'

'In our village'

'In your village? I think you are mistaken.'

'No, I am not mistaken. You used to stay in our village then. I was quite a small kid then. Barely ten.'

'What I was doing in your village?' Ron asked in a light, flippant tone.

'You were then trying to build a barrage over the Dikrong river.'

'What? A barrage? Where?'

'Over the Dikrong river.'

Ron suddenly felt as if the trees around him were reeling around his head.

Memories flooded back. Memories of the long-forgotten early days of their armed organization. Kumbang cast anxious glances at him, trying to gauge whether he was right or wrong in telling Ron.

Ron thought, *Well, here is a witness of those days! Days filled with excitement, of success and also of failure.* He recalled how kids used to crowd around them when they went to the villages in their strapping camouflage fatigues and armed with smart guns. The kids came and gaped at them and if you drove them away, they would scatter only to crowd around again. Kumbang must had been amongst them. He suddenly felt a surge of affection for Kumbang.

'Come, let's rest for a while,' Ron said, 'we have been walking since morning. Let's sit under that tree.'

Ron glanced at Kumbang and wondered, *What does he know? How much about those times of dreams, idealism…?* Ron took several deep breaths in the clear mountain air. Then he decided to tell Kumbang about those times.

'At that time,' Ron started, 'our organization had undertaken a series of programmes of social work. In different places roads were built, dykes and bunds were constructed, embankments were repaired or built for flood protection… and so on. The aim was to rouse the people, to unite and organize them and with their power, to build up beneficial public works. It was an effort to bring about mass mobilization. We would ask the people what work they wanted done in their area. The people would tell us and we would select one or two projects. We tried to involve people, to take the help of their voluntary labour.'

Kumbang said excitedly, 'I also participated in those social service programmes!'

'Did you? Tell me what you did? How did you do it?'

'First we went to help in the construction of an embankment on the bank of the Dikrong river. Everyone from our village went there. The day before, the gun-toting youths had come to our village and told us that everyone above sixteen years of age must work the next day!'

'Then what happened?'

'The next day, the gun-carrying boys again came at daybreak and gave us orders to leave the village with them and go to the site where work had to be done. They said everyone should bring their own implements—hoes, daos and spades along with baskets to carry soil. "Take all the implements needed!" they shouted. "Nobody can stay back. Everyone has to work or be punished!" So we all went.'

'But you were not sixteen years old at the time?'

'But we boys who were below the age specified also went with the men and women of the village.'

'What did you do there?'

'The gun-toting boys showed us how the work had to be done. They made us form different groups and allotted work. We kids helped the adults.'

'Those young boys, the gun-carrying boys, did they also work shoulder-to-shoulder with the people?' Ron asked.

'No, they marched from place to place and supervised the work. Once they beat up a few persons who had stopped working and took a break to smoke. There was a huge ruckus at that time.'

'Oh, I see,' Ron said slowly. Uncomfortable, he suddenly felt he would be relieved if he could change the topic.

'The person who was given the responsibility to feed the people soaked gram during the ongoing work used only two sacks of gram though he was asked to use three sacks. One sack just disappeared.'

Ron interrupted, 'I am feeling hungry, Kumbang. June has given us some cooked food, hasn't she? Let's eat.'

Thick unleavened bread, sugar and a little leftover marmot curry from last night was their feast. Ron could convince the leader to allow only four days for this ongoing expedition. So June had given them rotis to tide them over one meal every day. They had brought uncooked rice and lentils too. *But she doesn't understand*, Ron thought, *the rotis will become hard after some time and if the valley below is humid they will turn mouldy too. No use telling her.*

The memories of those days in the first days of the insurgency streamed through Ron's mind while he and the young boy were eating.

He remembered a sparkling blue sky above, a cool refreshing breeze that ruffled his hair and the slight nip of cold. In the morning, the distant bamboo thickets were covered with a light veil of mist. 'Kahua' had blossomed madly on the sandbanks of both sides of the Dikrong river, creating an undulating sea of white all around. Ron was standing on the bank of the Dikrong with a few of his colleagues.

One man in the group was pointing to the river and was excitedly shouting and gesticulating wildly. 'Look, look, there is the mouth!' the man was saying. 'That is the mouth of the main channel of the Dikrong river. Can you make it out? The river used to flow this way. But then it changed its course…'

'Changed its course?'

'Yes, changed its course. The main channel was blocked at that point. The ground rose and blocked it, probably as a result of the great earthquake of the 1950s. No one can be very sure now, but it did change its course.'

The man was jabbing the air with his finger.

'Look, look at the deep furrow-like impression. There—a little distance from where we are standing on this high ground—try to follow it with your eyes. You will see the deep depression, the wide furrow, extending for a long way. You can very well make it out. You can see the banks on both sides. The smell of the river still pervades the furrow. Yeah, the smell of the river. This was the old, original channel of the Dikrong river!'

Ron could see that through the elevated land awash with

the feathery 'Kahua' grass was a depression that looked like the dry bed of a dead river.

Yes, the dry bed of a dead river,

'The river flowed through this channel. It you go a little forward you will still find water at places! Water covered by water hyacinth and other aquatic plants. The channel still exists, from end to end several miles long.'

'Several miles long?'

'At this point the earth rose, possibly due to an earthquake and blocked the river. And the main river started flowing in a new channel. The flowing water rolled over the land through the natural depressions, churning the land, digging new ways and ultimately creating a new channel. Now the river flows through this channel. This old channel died. During the rains when the flow increases, a small part still flows through this and the old folks say that when the river didn't cause erosion or erode the banks, destroying paddy fields and habitations, it did not try to change its course frequently.'

'And now?' Ron asked.

'Now the river erodes the banks,' the man jabbed his forefinger into the air for emphasis. 'It has now threatened to erode the 'Bihupuria' town. In a year or two it will take a good bite of the town. Mark my words, it will erode the entire town.'

Ron focused his attention back to the present. It was already afternoon!

The air had become cooler, more pleasant, and the evening mist had started to float in the distance. Ron suddenly remembered a couplet from the epics his grandmother used to recite to him.

'*The sky is pure, transparent it has become.*
    The waters and the clouds disappeared
Oh, so pleasant the air fragrant.
    The breeze blowing all the time...'

                                        (Shankaradeva)

It was early autumn when on the banks of the Dikrong, Ron had tried to pay attention to the man.

'What do you suggest we should do now?' Ron had asked.

'Now?' The man had paused for a while. Then ceasing to gesticulate, he said, 'What we have to do is that we have to construct a barrage over the present channel of the Dikrong river, dig out the blocked mouth of the old one and thus divert the river, making it flow again in its original channel. In this way, the river will again flow by its ancient path. And once it happens, the 'Bihupuria' town and this wide area will be spared from devastating floods and erosion. The town will be saved.'

'How do you propose to do it?'

The man looked at the river for some time and then stated simply, 'In December and January, the flow in the river will become a trickle. Only one or two small channels will remain. Then we will construct a barrage by driving four parallel lines of stout bamboo posts from one bank to the other. Between these posts driven deep into the river bed at a distance of 3 to 4 feet, we shall put sand bags. We'll need thousands of sand bags, even a hundred thousand. Over this we shall pile soil dug from the blocked mouth of the old channel. We will make embankments at the banks for some distance. That will do it!'

'It was a grand dream, Kumbang!' Ron exclaimed after telling him the story of the Dikrong river project started by the organization.

Kumbang remained silent.

'Kumbang!' Ron called again,

'Yes, sir.'

'You didn't say anything.'

'About what?'

'About the grand dream of diverting the Dikrong river.'

'What happened to the project afterwards?'

'We had started digging bamboo stakes into the river bed, but at that time the military operation—Operation Bajrang—was launched. All the work had to be stopped because we had to go into hiding.'

'I see,' Kumbang said softly. 'It was a dream for some, but a nightmare for others.'

'Why? Why do you say that?' Ron asked.

'Do you know, sir, some miles downstream from the area where the old channel's mouth was blocked, was the village of my grandfather. My mother grew up there before her marriage. It was a large Mishing tribal village. It was right on the banks of the old river bed. The paddy fields, the fishing beels of the villagers were all in that river bed.

Still further downstream, there were villages of fisherman and other communities. Everyone cultivated fields in the bed of the dead Dikrong.'

Ron sat up straight. He heard Kumbang's words with increasing incredulousness.

'What would have happened if the river was diverted and made to flow in the old channel? Several villages, and the paddy fields of hundreds of families, would have been washed away, especially during the rains and floods. Isn't it so?'

Ron heard him out.

'So our people of the Mishing villages, people of the Kaibarta fisherfolk villages had vehemently opposed the construction of the barrage and diversion of the river.'

'How did you come to know about all this, Kumbang?'

'My grandfather's house was right there. Grandpa came to our village searching for land nearby to shift his household to. Other people also did that. You didn't know about these occurrences, sir?'

'No,' Ron shook his head, 'we didn't.'

'The villagers had openly told the boys from the organization about their opposition to the project. They had said, "Don't ever come here any more, never set foot in our village"…'

22

'Why did you join the organization, Kumbang?'

They were resting inside the forest. Ron was reclining against an earthen mound with his hands clasped behind his head. Kumbang was sitting nearby silently, cleaning the two small birds he had felled with his sling shot. He carefully plucked them, feather by feather, gutted them, rubbed salt inside and outside and lastly, wrapped the bird in a tight bundle of leaves and bound it up with string. Ron was looking at the process with fascination. Kumbang lifted his head, smiled and said. 'I hope the meat stays fresh till we reach the cave.' Then he added, 'In these mountain valleys edible plants or fruits are scarce, there are very few birds in the trees and no fish in the streams.'

'I don't think fish can live in such cold water. Moreover, these are quite seasonal streams and the river fish can't swim up to these heights,' Ron said.

However, they had found a small clump of banana trees at one place. They cut up a few trees, peeled away the outer layers and brought out the juicy inner core. They made foot-long pieces and took those with them to use as vegetables. After Kumbang chewed a piece, he spat it out and said, 'This is too alkaline. June will have to soak them in salt water for a long time to remove the alkaline taste.'

'You must tell her,' Ron had said. That was their last night in the forest. The leader had ordered them to return on the fourth day if not the third. After he had seen that there was barely anything edible to get from the forest, Ron also wanted to go back early. They didn't find any trace of human habitation, nor did they see any game there. The only indication of any animal life were the wolf howls they heard one night, indicating that a pack was roaming in the forest at some distance. The only luck they had was when Kumbang could kill six birds. The first two they had eaten roasted over a small fire, while Kumbang had salted the remaining four to take to the cave.

After climbing up a stiff mountain face on their way back, they had rested near a small mound where Ron put that question to Kumbang, 'Why did you join the organization?'

Ron found Kumbang quite pleasant and interesting. *The boy knows how to behave*, Ron thought, *never speaking unless spoken to but never holding back when asked a question.*

'It just happened,' Kumbang replied with a smile.

'There are not many boys from your tribe in our organization. Why is that so?'

'It happened gradually due to some events, but it all started with....' Kumbang paused.

'Started with what?'

'It started with a cache of arms.'

Ron sat up from his reclining position 'What cache of arms?'

Ron heard with increasing incredulity the story Kumbang narrated.

'There is a ferry-crossing in the Subansiri river. Have you seen that? Yes? I know you must have. Though now a bridge spans the river in the north, in the south big boats— machine boats, these are called—use the ferry. A bunch of local rogues rule the ferry-crossing world. Without their permission, no boats or goods can cross the river. These rogues are in turn controlled by organizations of the local tribal youths. One day, a few boxes were transported by boat—they were sealed but were very heavy. The rogue-controlled loading gang demanded triple fees for carrying them. The two boys who were in change of the boxes first refused and there was a terrible altercation, the boys and the rogues coming to blows. Then they settled for a sum. The ferry was very crowded that day. While the porters unloaded the boxes, they dropped one. It broke and the loaders saw that it was full of arms. A tremendous commotion followed and the loaders seized the boxes. The two boys who had brought the boxes simply melted into the crowd. The tribal youth organization which controlled the rogues and the porters then took charge of the boxes and secreted them away.'

Ron whistled softly. He had heard about the incident though he was not involved in it personally. He also knew that the leader was involved. Yes that much Ron knew, but he didn't tell Kumbang about it.

'What happened then?'

'The underground organization which owned the arms now closed in, searching for them. They accused the tribal youth organization of spiriting them away and threatened them with dire consequences.'

'Why was the relationship between the underground and the tribal youth organizations so strained?' Ron asked.

Kumbang paused, then said slowly, 'That's a long story. I will tell you the main point. Previously, the underground was very active amongst the tribals. They got shelter, support and food in the villages. The youth was also drawn to them, some even joined them. But then small incidents began happening, like intimidation, scoldings, misunderstandings. The boys even spoke out against the tribal practice of brewing rice wine in every household! These attacks on their customs made the tribals apprehensive. Ultimately, the underground organization started confiscating the guns of the tribals, which angered them immensely—as you know, after the possession of an elephant, a gun is the greatest status symbol for a tribal household. They united, organized themselves, confronted the underground men and told them not to set foot in the tribal villages again. The youth, backed by the older and the rich folks, floated an organization and took active part in it. The rest you know, don't you?'

Ron silently nodded then asked, 'What happened to the cache of arms and when did you get into the picture?'

'There were intense negotiations night after night and I came in during that time. I became a sort of messenger between the tribal youth organization and the underground. I was chosen to do the job because the underground leaders stayed in a house in the nearest non-tribal village and the son of the owner of that house was one of my closest friends. We visited each other quite often.'

'So you knew what was happening?' Ron said.

'The connection was not clear, in the sense that it wasn't really included in the meetings,' Kumbang replied. 'There were intense negotiations. I didn't know all the details, but I knew the arms were returned. There were promises that the two groups would not interfere in each other's activities, that much I know.'

'And then?'

'Then the police got scent of the whole thing. The arms had by then been shifted out safely and the leaders had gone. And once the police operation started in earnest, the tribal youth leaders also scattered. I did not know the police had swung into action. Probably a police informer in my friend's village or even in our village had pointed me out to the police. Shortly after, I was arrested.'

Ron gave out a short dry laugh and said, 'It always happens like that.'

'After keeping me in custody for a night the police let me go home that time, but after that, whenever there were police operations, whenever they came to our villages, they would arrest me. It happened four times and the last two times, they even beat me up badly. I became afraid that the police was trying to frame me in some case. So I decided to flee from home, leave the village and go away to another place. People usually flee to the towns or to the city of Guwahati. I decided I would leave the state altogether and seek a job in Goa. Why Goa? I had long heard about it, about how beautiful it is, about the beaches. One of my closest friends had been there. I heard stories about it from him and always wanted to go there. So this time I decided Goa would be my destination.'

'Then what happened?'

'On the way, I met the leader of the underground who had come for negotiations in the missing arms case. He recognized me and invited me to go with him so I changed my mind. And here I am now in the mountain cave, ha ha.' Kumbang laughed loudly.

Ron, however, remained silent with his hands clasped behind his head and his eyes closed. Kumbang glanced at him and then became silent.

'I also want to go to Goa,' Ron suddenly said, startling Kumbang. He still had his eyes closed. 'I have seen the sea, been on a ship in the ocean, seen the mountains, but I have never been to Goa. I want to go to its beaches, which I have heard so much of! I want to lie in the golden sands of the Calangute beach. I have seen the beach of Puri, where the sand is silvery. I have heard that the sands of Calangute are golden. Lying there with my eyes closed, I want to hear the sound of waves breaking into the shore, the call of lonely seagulls, the strumming of a guitar from a distant shack at night....'

Kumbang didn't say anything. He looked at Ron's face, transfixed.

Then Ron opened his eyes, his characteristic shy smile lighting up his face, and said, 'After we leave the cave, let us go to Goa for a few days, you and me. We will walk the beaches and imagine a big ship of Portugal sailing in the sea, all its sails unfurled and its pennants flying.'

Kumbang was so excited, he didn't know what to say. After a pause he said. 'Promise? Promise you will take me to Goa with you!'

Ron extended his hand and gave Kumbang a high-five, 'It's a promise, Kumbang, it's a promise.'

23

THAT VERY DAY, the leader suddenly asked Ron, 'Where did you get into the arms scene? In Malacca?'

The question startled Ron. It was totally unexpected.

They were warming themselves in the afternoon sun, just outside the cave mouth, Ron sitting on a rock and the leader on his stretcher, which he fondly called his sunning chair.

'You mean the ship and the sea cargo thing.'

'What else? My memory is starting to play tricks with me. I had arranged the whole operation, fixed the roles of people for different legs of it, but now I seem to forget whom I had put where. You were in the last leg of it? Isn't it so?'

'Yes, in Malacca. I oversaw the transfer of the cargo from the small ship they call a sampan.'

'Yes, I remember that,' the leader said. 'Malacca—that's the main area of the sea pirates.'

Ron said, 'Yes, it was quite an adventure.'

'It's a narrow strait that carries a huge volume of the world's shipping. Hundreds of big ships ply through it daily. It's the only way that connects the Indian Ocean with the Pacific. Small ships would number in thousands, those that sail the coastal waters. It's only natural that it will be infested with pirates. They prey on the commercial ships that pass through the straits.'

'You were in Bangkok at that time?' Ron asked.

The leader chuckled. 'I gave the impression that I was in Bangkok, but I was in a different place, in Singapore.'

Lately, he had started to talk with Ron quite often. He would talk about various incidents and also about organizational matters.

'There are certain things you must know. Maybe you've already heard about them, because you had participated in all the activities, but it's impossible to know many details unless you are told. In secretive underground organizations like ours, circumstances and issues are never discussed openly. The information given is very selective and scarce. You only know about the part where you were involved. Isn't it so?'

'That's true.'

'I feel now you need to know more about certain important matters, at least to the extent of what I know myself. In future, you will have to shoulder still greater responsibilities of the organization…' He had left the rest unsaid.

When he talked with Ron on these matters, he ensured that no one was within earshot.

'What did you do in Malacca, Ron?'

'The crates came from three sources. All of them were carried by small ships, big boats really. They are called sampans, Chinese sampans, and are very efficient crafts. One even had a sail.'

'Yes, very effective crafts, no doubt about it. They ply from Vietnam, Thailand, the Philippines, Indonesia, right up to Akiyab in Burma. Thousands of them. Also from the South China Sea to the Bay of Bengal.'

'Some are quite modern, like miniature ships.'

'Yes, I had visited a shipyard where they are built. They are all at a little distance from the main area and always better approached by sea. Surrounding these shipyards are the cavernous warehouses that, in addition to all other goods, also store the materials we need,' the leader chuckled.

'Where are the arms procured from?'

'From arms merchants.'

'How did you contact them?'

'It was very difficult. It took me one year to get a proper contact. It's not that there are shops where you can walk in and say "I want this I want that, what's the price?" You have to spend sizeable amounts of money even to get contacts. These arms merchants are Chinese men from Malaysia, Singapore, Hong Kong…to first contact them, you need the right connections to get to them.'

'And the arms? Do they come from China?'

'Mostly not, maybe some, but the bulk come from areas of the world where there had been major wars, like Iraq, Iran, Kuwait, Afghanistan, or areas where the state structure had broken down like the USSR and Eastern Europe. There are special agents who gather all that's available. Then there are others who transport them, both new and second-hand arms, and there are still others who store them in unmarked warehouses, or sometimes even in the holds of ships and sampans in the high seas. It's a big, well organized and dangerous market.'

The leader warmed up to the topic. Ron listened.

'You know, in the USSR and Eastern Europe, after the fall of the old regimes, arms were sold as metal scraps, not by the owners or the government, but by anybody, any charlatan who could do it. And there were even a few Indian merchants who purchased them as scrap, then shipped them off and resold them to arms dealers.'

'I see, but why from Europe to here?'

'Well, it's a question of demand and supply. Supplies come from places where things are available and come to areas where there is a demand. Simple economics. In every step, yes every step, you have to pay an advance. You first state what your requirements are, after which they investigate, taking some time to find out about you. Once they are satisfied, they contact the buyers and tell them where to view the stash. For that buyers have to pay again. Then they examine the arms and select what they need. Whatever they select, will be greased and packed, locked in crates and the key handed over. When the necessary payment is made, the merchandise is supplied to predetermined places. In your case, they delivered the arms to your sampan and you took the delivery.'

'Yes, as instructed, I took delivery of thirty-two cases, which were transferred to my sampan in the high seas.

Then we set sail and delivered it to a ship just outside the straits. My duty ended there. I went back by the sampan, reached the shore and went to Bangkok,' Ron said.

'I didn't make contact with you but I was receiving all the news, right up to when the arms were loaded into the last ship and your departure. The whole process is quite well organized, really. So long as one goes on paying money on time, the transactions would be carried out without any problem.'

'Yes, it looked like it,'

'It was. My duty also was to ensure that the arms were put safely into the last ship. From there on, others looked after the consignment. You can't imagine, Ron, what tensions I had those days. It involved a huge sum and it was very important for our organization. So I followed it up to its safe landing and was relieved when I got the news that you had arrived in Bangkok safely and the arms had landed in the assigned place without any problem.'

'Why did you keep track of the ship to the very end up to the landing of the consignment, when your assigned duty finished with its loading and setting sail?' Ron suddenly asked.

The leader was startled by Ron's question. Ron himself was no less surprised.

Why did he ask it, knowing fully well that it would unsettle the leader? He himself had taken a lot of trouble to get together the consignment of arms in the murky waters of Malacca. He had faced real danger, lived through endless periods of anxiety and uncertainty. And when later, he got to know that a large part of that armed cache was discovered and seized by Bangladeshi authorities after it had landed in Chittagong, he had felt dejected and defeated. At the same time, a whiff of suspicion also entered his mind—how could it have happened?

'You are asking why I followed the ship up to its final destination even though my formal duty had ended?' the leader asked in a low, calm voice. 'There are reasons for it. That last ship also contained our own people, you didn't know about that. I had a responsibility for them—everything was organized by me to ensure safety, while others were assigned to see that it reached the destination safely. I couldn't shirk from my responsibility. Moreover….'

'Moreover what?'

'Sometimes these sampans disappear in the sea without any trace,' the leader said.

'Are you talking about sinking? The sampan I used was very old, with paint peeling and patches of rust showing through. I myself was also quite worried.'

'No. Sinking would have been an accident. I am not speaking about that.'

'Then?'

'This kind of shipping, which means carrying contraband, is controlled by ruthless criminals. At their signal, sometimes the ship would cut off all contacts in the high seas, sail to another destination and unload its cargo there. Then the whole ship would vanish. It would be taken to a secret destination, repainted, renamed and would sail under different documents. You would find no trace of the old ship.'

Ron kept silent. So long he had been looking constantly at the leader, who had been speaking with his eyes shut. Then he opened his eyes and looked at Ron for a long time as if he was trying to size him up. Then keeping his steady gaze on Ron, the leader slowly said, 'Our arms were not unloaded in Chittagong.'

Ron also held his gaze, waiting to hear more.

'The boxes were unloaded from the ship well outside the territorial waters of Bangladesh into small fishing trawlers, which carried them to the port of Cox's Bazar. They were stored in Cox's Bazar. I was greatly worried about this last leg of the operation.'

'And they were seized in Cox's Bazar?' Ron's voice had a tinge of bitterness.

'Yes, when the last lots were taken out from the warehouse by truck, the largest part.'

The leader had closed his eyes again. He was breathing deeply as if he was panting. The conversation had put a lot of pressure on him for sure as he revealed what had really happened. Ron had known that the seizure of the arms had happened under mysterious circumstances, even though many precautions were taken. Despite that, the arms were lost in suspicious circumstances....

'I always said that the arms should never be stored even in a secret unmarked warehouse. The moment they reached land they should have been divided into different lots and moved. Such things should always be kept in motion, should never be stationary, but my counsel was not heeded.' The leader droned on without opening his eyes.

Ron remained silent.

Some memories surfaced like bubbles. So much of effort, so much money had gone in vain. And the arms were seized in a country that was disposed to friendship. Had it been in India, would it have been a different matter? Ron remembered the discussions that had occurred within the organization.

Had the arms arrived, the organization would have been greatly strengthened. But the pressing question was, would the arms have empowered a person within the organization? And so much so that he would have become unassailable? Nobody could have challenged him then! Was this the root of the mystery?

There was gossip. There was talk of someone from inside leaking the news about the arms. Could it have been true? Such rumours spread swiftly through the grapevine, acquired a life force of their own. Ron remembered that it was not only discussed in whispers within the organization but found its way to the press, the media and rebounded back to the organization. Suspicion was born.

The needle of suspicion had pointed to the leader also.

Ron wearily looked towards the leader. He still had his eyes shut, but his lips were moving silently as if he was mumbling something. Ron looked up at the sky. The afternoon sun had softened and the air had become cold. It was time to move the leader in. He got up and called the boys.

'Today the cold has come early,' he said loudly, standing near the leader.

The leader opened his eyes and looked at Ron in surprise. Then he understood and said,

'Yes, yes, let's move inside. It looks like the sky is starting to freeze, isn't it? I am feeling the cold in my bones even under these blankets. Yes, the sky is not like the other days…'

A large fire was built inside the cave. Despite the cave mouth being barred, the cold slowly seeped in through the gaps. The fire threw its dancing shadows on the cave wall and the shadows of June and Kumbang, who were moving near it for the evening cooking, looked like shadows of ghosts on the walls. They observed Ron looking intently at the leader who had again closed his eyes and had possibly gone to sleep, but didn't say anything.

Ron was still thinking about the lost arms.

Yes, it definitely looked like some inside job.

Ron was getting more and more convinced that someone had been behind the disappearance of the arms. The efforts of so many boys in the organization had gone in vain, not to speak of the dangers they were exposed to! The seized arms had vanished without a trace and Ron had often asked himself who was responsible. *The police? The army? The Intelligence Bureau?* After that incident so many leading cadres had lost their positions, so many were disgraced. He didn't want to think more about it.

The light and shadow of the fire was playing on the face of the sleeping leader.

Ron remembered the conversation he had. The slight pauses, the controlled agitation in the leader's voice and expression, the sudden startled look and measured tones that the leader had used from time to time, all these small signs which he noticed today! What did they mean? Although he couldn't put a finger to anything definite, Ron was becoming more and more convinced; convinced that his suspicion was true!

He suddenly felt his heart beating rapidly inside his chest.

June had stoked the fire, its glow reflecting on the leader's face.

Am I looking at the face of a traitor? Ron thought suddenly. He couldn't divert his gaze from the face of the sleeping leader though he wanted to... *Is this the face of a betrayer?* Ron felt his mouth turning dry. He felt as if insects had entered his brain, buzzing agitatedly. The face of a traitor—*the face of Judas?*

24

Ron had nightmares that night. He tossed and turned in bed. Feeling the cold creeping up, he wrapped his rug tightly around himself and tried to go to sleep. Whenever he drifted into sleep, the nightmares returned. They were disjointed dreams about an incident he would never forget.

The turbid waters of the Malacca strait flowed in a twisting manner and his sampan rolled constantly. When the sampan had sailed near the coast, Ron had seen a small river emptying itself into the strait. The water was orange-red and it had coloured the strait waters red for a long distance. A red river?

He had asked the captain about it.

'There is heavy logging upstream,' he had replied. 'They are practically digging up the forests and the damaged land is being washed to the sea.'

There were Rohingia Muslims amongst the crew of the sampan and also khalasis from Chittagong, or Chattogram as they called it. The previous night somebody had sung a 'Bhatiali' song in a beautiful voice. Ron wanted to find out who had sung the song, but he was under strict instructions not to let anybody know where he was from. In that silent night, in the rolling sampan in the strait of Malacca, the

'Bhatiali' song felt so close to his heart, like the melody of the 'Oinitam' which Kumbang sang in a sad voice in the lonely afternoons of the cave.

The waters were rough on the last day when the sampan he was in approached the sea and the ship anchored out there. Purple-violet clouds floated in a nearly black sky with a dirty half-moon making its occasional appearances. The sampan had approached the ship silently. There was no welcoming or warning hoots of the ship's sirens from either side. It was in those rough waters that the thirty-two crates had been transferred from the sampan to the ship by a creaky ship crane. Towards morning, the whole operation ended and Ron got the receipt of the thirty-two crates from the mate of the ship, who was also a Rohingia from Bangladesh. He was forbidden to board the ship.

The whole incident was like a bizarre nightmare, with a hint of unreality. It was a weird, frightening, storm-tossed night. Then the sampan was cut from its mooring to the ship and pushed away. The sampan moved away and the ship was soon lost, invisible in the early morning grey mist. Ron had returned to the sampan. After the mentally and physically tiring night, he had felt drained. He fell into a fitful sleep and when he got up after several hours it was calm, the sea and the sky a brilliant blue. When he came out to the bridge of the sampan he saw large brown oil slicks floating lazily on the surface of the water. He had felt ravenously hungry.

Large tankers and container slips were travelling lazily in the distance. The wake of the large ships was so strong that it caused the sampan to roll from quite a distance. The large *oil tankers were so huge that they couldn't enter the harbour. They had to anchor on the high seas from where small tankers transferred the crude oil.*

The night before he was to disembark from the sampan on the coast of Thailand, a storm lashed the sea. Large waves tossed the sampan, which was as fragile as a paper boat, rolling dangerously. Ron had felt sick and frightened. It must have shown in his face because he remembered that the Khalasis, the Malay mates and the Chinese sailors had laughed at him. The Malay mate who knew a little English shouted near his ear, 'This is not a dangerous storm, don't be afraid. It's just a patch of rough sea.'

Ron felt a shudder even in his dream. Several times, he woke up with a start from the intensely vivid and disturbing dream. The face of the leader floated up before him. Light and shadows from the dancing flames played in his face, illuminating his profile, detailing the strong jaw with the cleft, the bushy eyebrows… Whose was that sphinx-like face? Did it belong to a large hairy spider sitting in the centre of the web with the filaments spreading all around! Or did it belong to Judas?

The cold increased every day. Except in the daytime when the sun shone, the cold was numbing. The wind that blew from the mountainside stung like needles at times and the mist also rose early, greyer and thicker, adding a deep gloom to the surroundings.

Ron could make out that everybody was worried. The

thought of leaving the cave and going down to the warmer plains of Assam was on everyone's mind. No one spoke about it openly but Ron could see the questions on their faces.

One day June brought up the topic.

The leader was asleep. Ron, Pradip, Kumbang and June sat at one side of the fire.

'The weather is getting cold,' she started. 'Snowfall may not be far away. What are you planning about our next step? Isn't it time we left the mountains?'

Ron hadn't replied immediately. He asked, 'What do you think?'

'I am only thinking about the patient,' June said.

'Well…' Ron waited for her to continue.

'My own feeling is…' June had started cautiously. 'His condition is not going to improve much. Possibly some other kind of treatment is required. If we stay the long winter here…' Her voice wavered and she looked at everyone, 'His condition may deteriorate in this chilly stony cave,' she finished in a whisper.

They had remained silent for a long time.

'You are right, we have to move,' Ron said emphatically. 'Yes, we need to move, I think this is only a cold spell that has come early, but we shall have to take a decision soon, say in a week's time. All of you must think about it, think of what we need to do to move, also…' he had paused, then went on, 'we have to think about the other alternative also. What if we have to pass the winter months in this cave? What then? That would be our plan number two.

We have to be realists and think about this plan two also. Everybody must keep that in mind.'

Nobody said anything.

I have always liked snow. I really enjoyed the snowfall in the camp, June told herself, following a slow train of thought. The first time she saw snow falling, she had been nearly delirious with joy and excitement. The snowflakes immediately melted and disappeared when they fell on the ground or when people tried to catch them in their palms. Most camp inmates had seen snow for the first time in their life.

The next morning, the whole world had turned white and the snowbanks shone in the bright sunlight. June and other camp inmates had stared in wonder, practically speechless. Then somebody raised his voice in a 'Hip Hip Hurray' and everyone responded.

She had always revelled in the cold and snow. The freedom from sweat, the pleasurable warmth of fire and the camaraderie of closed groups—June had loved them all.

But now the cold depressed her. She felt that the cave was also changing with the cold. It was becoming more and more inhospitable. *The cave has become like a prison*, she thought. And inside that prison she felt that she was a prisoner of another jail, a special jail for herself.

Though she was now able to go out of the cave in the afternoon after her chores were done, she was still not satisfied. It was as if a favour had been granted to her because she had not been assigned duties where she could go out like the boys did on duty, to bring grass and wood for the fuel store, or patrolling, on sentry duty.

When this realization dawned, June again felt restless. She wanted to speak to someone, but who could she confide in? If she talked to Pradip he wouldn't understand or he would just joke about it. She didn't know how Ron would react. He might not say anything or might snap back at her.

Cooking had become the most hateful job for her. She had started to detest it. She would prepare the leader's food carefully, but for the others she would just make a few thick hard rotis and lentil curry with dried chillies or simply rice and dal. The boy who helped her to knead the flour would get a tongue lashing from her. When the boys realized that June was again in one of her foul moods, they avoided her. This is turn made her angrier.

At last she decided to talk to the leader, but couldn't decide how she should do it.

It was the leader who first asked her when they were alone, 'June, what is the matter? You seem unhappy.'

She was startled by the question. Then she decided to seize the opportunity as it presented itself, 'Yes, sir, I am really unhappy about the way I am treated here,'

She sat down near the leader.

'Why? What has happened?' The leader became anxious.

June rubbed her eyes. She was not crying, but in a spontaneous reaction, her hands went to her eyes and she rubbed them.

'Don't cry, June, don't cry', the leader said.

'I am not crying,' she said but didn't remove her hands from her eyes. She was feeling nervous.

'I won't be able to bear it if you cry,' the leader said. 'Tell me what the matter is.'

'I am feeling humiliated.'

'Why ? Why?'

'I feel I am unwanted, like a prisoner. I am not able to take it lightly though I am trying. I feel as if I am being treated as a second-grade person within our little nine-member group.'

The leader looked distraught. He didn't know what to say. June didn't wait for him.

'I may be wrong, totally wrong. You know our circumstances here. I just want to tell you how I am feeling.'

'Please tell me. You don't have to worry whether you are right or wrong.'

'Do you remember how you gave me a great responsibility in the camp?

'Which responsibility?'

'I led a platoon of soldiers in the camp. We stood guard, did sentry duty, went on marches, gathered firewood, brought water, everything, every task that needed to be done in the camp.'

'I know, I remember.'

'Here, I am not allowed to work like the others. I'm kept away from some jobs.'

'What do you want, June?'

'I want to be treated equally like all others. Everybody

should be sharing duties, including looking after you. It's not happening here. This has really hurt my self-esteem. I feel humiliated since they think I'm only good enough to cook and clean. Maybe I have become a little emotional.'

'I will do something, don't worry. I will do something about it,' the leader said.

Both of them remained silent for some time. The leader said slowly, 'I know you all are having a tough time because of me. Don't think I do not understand it. What you all have done for me is incomparable. I have been able to give you nothing but troubles and worries. Wait, wait, wait, don't stop me. Let me speak. It's not easy to take care of an immobile man. Tell me honestly, June, don't you sometimes get fed up caring for me?'

'Yes, it happens,' June said candidly

'Thank you for telling the truth.'

'But when you go to sleep, it becomes quite boring. When I go out, leaving you behind, I constantly think about you. Then I come back to be near you.'

The leader looked at June with shining eyes.

'Are you telling the truth, June?'

June moved forward a little and took the leader's hand between hers. 'It's true,' she whispered. 'I don't know whether it's right to tell you this or not...., but it is true.'

'You don't know, June, what happiness your words have given me.'

June remained silent.

'Oh, how I would like to take you home with

me. Now only my old father lives there with my handicapped sister. She looks after him, and she is so sensitive, she can understand nearly everything. If we can go away from here, I think will go and stay there with my father and sister.'

'Oh, how happy they would be to see you…'

25

A BLACK RAVEN sat on a branch on the top of a tall pine, its feathers gleaming in the afternoon sun.

Ron looked at the raven for a long time. He was on a grassy atoll nearby, lying on the ground. He was alone. He had come out of the back exit of the cave, through the gully-like depression, by the little streamlet that trickled down though it, crossing the toilets they had built in convenient nooks and reached the grassy atoll beyond which was a sloping area covered with old, gnarled pines and deodars.

The trees were ancient, with thick trunks, but looked somewhat stunted and misshapen. Probably the strong mountain winds that blew through the narrow valley had made them so. Such trees could bring a sense of disquiet and unease. And atop the tallest tree sat the black shiny raven like a sentinel.

Lying down on the ground, Ron looked at the sky above. It was a nondescript sky that day with wispy clouds. Ron clasped his hands to form a pillow under his head and gazed at the landscape absent-mindedly. The craggy mountains seemed unfriendly.

Where did I start and where have I come? Ron suddenly asked himself. *And how long have I been in this life? Oh, what a life! Can I call it anything else but a barren journey? A sterile river?* His thinking became disjointed. He tried to organize his thoughts, tried to marshal the points for and against barrenness, and the first reference point that came to his mind was 'Love.'

As soon as the word came to him, there was a sudden upheaval in his mind. He felt as if feelings, emotions, thoughts swirled within, and he became restless, and also exasperated.

I have experienced love in this journey. I have known what love is. I have discovered how elevating it is, how sublime it can be! And I have realized also two things along with it. The path I have consciously chosen for myself, this strife-torn, dangerous and uncertain path did not allow me to continue the beautiful relationship that developed. This is the first realization. And I have also understood that true love calls for sacrifice of the highest order, yes, this is my second realization. And therefore, for the sake of the woman I loved, I had to break off the relationship. I did not continue, but silently withdrew from it. What would have happened if I had continued that relationship? Oh, it would have brought more suffering, more pain to both of us. Nothing else. So it is better to suffer alone than to make the woman you love suffer too.

Ron had sincerely hoped at the time of breaking off the first flush of his emotional youthful love, that his beloved would be able to forget their relationship, come to terms with the break-up with the passage of time. He did, however, suffer from bouts of pain and twinges of remorse when, occasionally, memories floated in.

When, after a few years he discovered that she had remained unmarried all these years, he was greatly disturbed.

The life I have chosen… it was my conscious decision, he repeated to himself. *It does not allow any marriage, any settling down. And she is not the type of girl who would have consciously chosen to lead this type of life.* These thoughts had been swirling around in his mind for a long time and had become quite stale—and he knew how inadequate they were.

He felt restless, sat up on the grassy mound and then stretched out again.

He remembered their frantic lovemaking and it made him cringe, curl up in an involuntary spasm. He drew his legs up to his chest, then straightened them, turned to one side and closed his eyes. When after some time he opened his eyes, he saw the raven was still perched on the top branch, turning its head from side to side.

He tried to drive away all those thoughts about the past from his mind and to think about something else, something more immediate and urgent.

The raven leapt from the branch and flew away silently. Ron looked after it with a sort of longing. *The past is past*, he thought, *it's not going to come back. The reality now is the cave, the cave!*

Ron always had a premonition that something was going to happen while he was in the camp.

Yes, the noose was being tightened.

The border patrolling had become very heavy and it became increasingly difficult to pass through. Encounters increased, so did the casualties.

Food procurement was dwindling. Their stores inside the camp were adequate but it became increasingly difficult to procure food from the village sources.

The middlemen disappeared.

And the little village shops where they could buy milk powder, baby food and other small items like needles and thread, wool and knitting needles in the past, either ran out of stock or they couldn't get the goods even with an advance payment. The only refrain was always, 'It is not available—everything comes from India, but those supplies have stopped.'

They could go only to the small village shops. They couldn't go to the nearby small town. That was part of the understanding with the local government in Bhutan.

Ron had recognized the symptoms. Something was surely brewing.

The leader was not ready to even acknowledge it. He had placed his faith in diplomacy, talks with the local government, on interaction with the local authorities.

When the attack came, it was devastating

Who would tolerate a foreign armed group establishing an armed camp in their country? They might have been weak to start with, but didn't stay so. There was always the might of India ready to extend help to uproot the rebels.

Ron had even raised the need for a contingency plan.

There were many women, children and even a few old men in the camp, some comrades, some camp followers.

If only the others in the leadership had heeded to my cautioning, Ron thought bitterly.

Now he had no idea where all those people in the camp were, where they had gone. How many escaped, how many got caught or were killed. And he had no way of knowing it in the immediate future.

Ron didn't want to think about it any more!

He sighed and curled up on his side.

He looked for the raven. It had disappeared. He saw two magpies strutting from place to place.

The only reality left now is the cave!

Ron was reluctant to return to the cave, but then realized bitterly that he had to do so. There was no alternative. He didn't want to think about the approaching winter, but there was no escape from it either.

He started to doze off.

Then he suddenly remembered another cave. A cave on a hill slope near one of their camps where he had buried one of his closest friends. A friend who could no longer bear the burden of life in the wilderness and had committed suicide.

You killed yourself, my friend, Ron thought dazedly, *and we have committed political suicide…*

An armed camp in a foreign county… that too, in such an open way as if they had already owned the land. Where were the masses that the communists so fondly mention … saying we have to live amongst the masses like fish in water, breathe the air they breathe, eat the food they eat, be one with them… gain their confidence, organize them, rouse them and then lead them….

Well, nothing of that sort happened, nor was it attempted. That route was not taken. They were not communists! They said they liberated people as well as territory, using tactics of terror like they had done in China or Russia, among other places. That was their path and motto.

It's no use dwelling on a past that's never going to come back. I should take a nap before going back to the cave, Ron told himself.

He felt a mantle of drowsiness covering him in a light embrace—and he was conscious of gently falling asleep.

And so he slept—slept and dreamed.

He dreamt of June.

26

DAY BY DAY, the sky became opaque.

The cold in the air was no longer pleasant, it had become biting. More than the physical discomfort, it became depressing. The greyness all around became like a heavy load that pressed down on them.

During their off-duty time, the boys no longer sat together, chatting or playing ludo with coloured pebbles and a wooden dice—carved by Kumbang and mostly throwing the number three up because it was a little crooked!

Now, whenever the boys got time off, they would sleep. They would go to their grass beds, unroll the rug, curl up under it and straight away go to sleep. Ron had stopped saying anything. In the evening, he would try to keep them awake by telling them various stories. There were no books or any training manual in the cave. Everything had been left in the destroyed camp. Ron had tried to recollect the instructions in those manuals and tried to talk about them to the boys. Soon he observed that they were not paying attention. They did try to stifle their yawns but their eyes closed. Ron stopped his attempts at educating them.

So they slept during off-duty time. Even June did.

In the bleak, dreary atmosphere June had a foreboding that something terrible was going to happen. She was really afraid and was struck by frequent unexpected palpitations.

Now, nobody wants to move out of the cave, she thought. It was a good thing that Ron had moved the sentry posts below the ledge of the cave for the night. At daytime, it was possible to stand for sentry duty at the old posts, but at night people could freeze to death there. Another good measure Ron had taken was to make the slits in the cave door smaller. It had greatly reduced the draught of cold air.

She went out one evening to the ledge, although it was terribly cold and wet.

A freezing wind laden with moisture swept down from the grey mountains, mountains enveloped in a thick mantle of mist. And at intervals, it swirled down along with the wind.

It was really cursed weather. The question now was of survival, surviving this winter. The leader had commented, 'I feel the winter is setting in early this year. It's quite unusual. The snowfall may be early also.' Yet nobody made any comment when he said that.

She looked into the sky. The greyish yellow pale moon floated into the gap created by the parting of the clouds above. The middle of the sky looked like a pond with the moon floating in it.

And then she heard it—faint, very faint at first. It was a long, sinuous wailing sound! *What's that?* June wondered. *Is it the wind or something else? No, no, it's not the wind.*

It's a wolf howling! And at that moment, three or four howls answered the first, then the howls stopped. The surrounding clouds closed in and obscured the moon.

She became frightened, an inexplicable fear. *This place is really becoming eerie*, she thought.

'What are you doing here?'

June was startled by the sudden question.

'Pradip?'

'Yes. I saw you coming outside. It's very cold here.'

'Yes, it's very cold, but the air is fresh.'

'Come inside. If you catch a cold and get feverish… that won't be a good thing.'

Ron also came out. He looked at them and said nothing.

Pradip said, 'I've asked June to move inside.'

'It feels very fresh here, don't you think?' Ron said.

'Yes,' June said eagerly. 'The moon came out for some time and during that time you know what? Two or three wolves howled.'

'When we went down we heard wolves howling from quite near. It's a small pack that's roaming this area, not more than five or six members.'

'How could you make out, sir?'

'From the number of howls, how many answers were given to the first call. Of course, there may be cubs that don't yet howl.'

After some time in the cold air, all three of then trooped inside silently.

The next day was the same, but even more bleak, dark and depressing.

June was on sentry duty in the morning shift. After her talk with the leader, Ron had given her sentry and outside duty just like the others, but not night duty. She was actually thankful for that but didn't say it. Cooking was now distributed to everyone, and June was very relieved at that. It felt really good to eat food cooked by others. Whenever she was not on sentry duty or had to go outside, she would insist on cooking the gruel for the leader herself.

She was shivering inside the dugout of the sentry post. *Only I am to be blamed for my plight*, she thought. *I can't grumble now.* She exhaled deeply, looking at the pattern her condensed breath created in the cold air.

She drew her gun near, careful to touch only the wooden parts, the handgrip below the barrel and the butt. The metal parts felt exceedingly cold. She didn't have gloves or mittens, nobody had, so she wrapped cotton rags around her hands. Through that, the exposed tips of her fingers felt numb. She had more than two hours to go before her sentry shift would be over.

Suddenly Kumbang materialized near the dugout.

'What? What are you doing here? It's not yet time for your shift!'

'I came early.'

'You didn't have to. Why, what has happened?'

'Sona burnt the rice while cooking. Nobody could eat it.'

'Where is Ron?'

'He is not there.'

'Did it stink?'

'To high heavens. The whole cave now smells of burnt rice.'

'What did the leader say?'

'Mercifully, he was asleep at that time, but when he smelt it, he became very angry. "It's sheer carelessness that led to wastage of food," he said. And do you know what he did? He ordered Sona's rice ration to be reduced till the loss is recovered.'

'Oh, oh.'

'In the camp he would have got a few lashes,' Kumbang said.

Both of them laughed uproariously. The laughter reverberated in the dugout, bouncing back on the rolling fog.

'Jump in,' June said, 'I am feeling very cold. Iciness is creeping up from the feet.'

Kumbang got inside the dugout

'Come, sit near me. We can keep each other warm.'

They sat together in the little plank inside the dugout, their voluminous padded jackets nearly touching each other. Their clothes had stiffened and became coated with grime because they had never been cleaned. The jackets smelled too, but they had become immune to the odour of their own, as well as others' jackets.

Kumbang noticed that through the stale sour smell of their unwashed garments wafted some other smell, like newly cut grass. *It must be coming from June*, Kumbang thought. *How strange, she has no cosmetics, cream or hair oil in the cave.* None of them did—they used ash from the fire for washing. *Then how is this faint fragrance like a mixture of flowers and freshly cut grass coming from her? Do all girls naturally smell nice?*

She became conscious that he was sniffing at her smell. She was menstruating. She knew that during such times many girls smell differently. *I hope he can't make that out*, she fervently thought.

They started talking.

'Tell me about your village.'

Kumbang launched into a graphic description of his village, its sylvan surroundings, the houses of the Mishing people built on stilts, the bright days, the moonlit nights and carefree life of the village.

'Do foxes howl there?'

'Foxes? There are several parties, not one. If one howled, another would start howling in a different place and ultimately, all the groups would howl. And then all the village dogs would start barking. There would be a great din.'

'I've heard Mishings love dancing. Does your village hold dance sessions?'

'Why not? Dance is an important part of tribal life—there are different dances for different occasions.'

'Did you dance too?'

'Of course I did. I am known as a good dancer.'

June looked at him in amusement with twinkling eyes. 'Really? But that is past?'

'Oh no. What do you people know about dancing?'

'Okay, tell me, what are the girls like?'

'Girls?'

'Yes, are they beautiful?'

'Sure, they are beautiful. Our village is known for its gorgeous girls. People from faraway places come seeking brides from our village. One very rich old man wanted to gift a double-barrel gun as a present to the father of a very beautiful girl.'

'A double-barrel gun!' June laughed loudly.

'You don't know what a gun means to a Mishing!'

'Forget about guns. Tell me one thing, did you have a lover?'

'No.'

'I see, nobody liked you, or you were just too young.'

'It is not like that.'

'Surely not, you never looked at any girl?'

'Of course I did.'

'Did you like anyone?'

'Several.'

'Only looked at them or touched them too?'

'Hey!' Kumbang shouted.

'Have you ever touched a girl'?

'What are you saying?'

'Slept with anyone?'

'Baideu, what are you saying?' Kumbang blushed furiously. 'Don't!'

'Have you seen the breasts of a girl? Touched them?'

Kumbang stood up, looking shocked.

'Sit down,' June said sharply. Then she repeated her question.

Confused, Kumbang sat down on the bench heavily.

June unzipped her jacket and rapidly unbuttoned her sweater and shirt. In a moment, she exposed her well-formed breasts. 'See,' she said.

Kumbong stole a glance, then looked away.

'Look at them,' June commanded.

He again stole a glance.

She snatched his hand, put it to her breast and said, 'Feel.'

She could feel the warmth of his palm. Kumbang did not withdraw his hand.

June waited, feeling the welcome warmth of his palm seeping in.

June could make out that Kumbang was breathing hard, and looking at her intently.

She removed his hand from her breast, smiled at him, ruffled his stiff hair and buttoned up her shirt and sweater as fast as she had unbuttoned them. Then zipping up her jacket, she said sweetly, 'I will go now. My sentry duty is nearly over. Keep the guard up.'

27

'I AM WORRIED,' June told Ron hesitantly.

He was sitting on a large loose stone on the ledge outside the cave door. His expression was sombre. June also observed that some deep worry lines had appeared on his face.

'Who isn't?' he gravely replied. 'Has anything new happened?'

'Our leader's health is slowly deteriorating. For the last three days he has been complaining of shooting pains going down his legs. Like electric currents, he says. It was there before also, but not so frequent and severe, and...'

'And what more?'

June was hurt by Ron's tone. It seemed he was suppressing irritation.

'A small sore has appeared on his lower back. It is still small, less than a centimetre, smaller than a five-rupee coin. And it's quite superficial, only the outer skin is affected. I made him lie on his side and we shall have to change his position quite frequently.'

Ron didn't say anything but he became glum. After some time, trying to bring an artificial naturalness into his voice, he said, 'What else can you do? Let us try our best to manage the situation. There is nothing much we can do, is there? Although, a doctor in our organization once taught me a procedure. He said that you can open up an antibiotic capsule and use the powder inside for dressing a wound. You can also do that. We have some antibiotic capsules in our drug box. Can you do that? It will prevent infection.'

'I can,' June also liked the suggestion.

They waited for some time.

'I am also worried about another thing,' Ron said. June stood closer to him. She wanted to hear Ron speak about his worries to her because she knew that he would never speak about them to anybody else. She sat on the ground near him, waiting for him to speak.

'I am worried after the hailstorm day before yesterday. It was such a heavy hailstorm. The whole meadow became white. Hail storms are unusual at this time of the year and after the storm, it has become colder. The temperature must have dropped by a couple of degrees. We'll have an early winter this year.'

June didn't say anything. She knew Ron hadn't finished yet.

'You were happy during the hailstorm. I saw you rejoicing, trying to catch hold of the hailstones that came jumping into the cave and putting them in your mouth.'

June silently smiled at his complaining tone. Yes, she was really delighted when the hailstorm broke. It had felt so fresh then—the air, which had been stifling, became light. Many stones came ricocheting into the cave and she had collected them, making everyone eat one. 'It's good to eat a hailstone from the first storm,' she had said. She even gave a tiny one to the leader who sucked it appreciatively.

June looked at Ron. He was serious again. 'We may have an early snowfall and it may be heavy too.'

'Well, everybody is waiting for your decision.'

'Decision regarding what?'

'Of making a move from the cave.'

'I am afraid.'

'Afraid of what?'

'Of many things. Whether our leader will be able to make it and whether we will be able to carry him on the stretcher. We don't know what is happening. We are totally cut off from the rest of the world. I tried to use the wireless, but nothing came except static sounds. Our frequencies might have been changed or....'

'Or what?' June had the distinct feeling that more than talking to her, Ron was actually talking to himself.

'Or... there is no one from our organization within the range of the wireless to respond. Our wireless network has been completely shattered. There are no more camps on this or the other side of the border any more. All our boys must have been scattered, many of them captured or dead.'

'We ourselves would have been dead by now if we hadn't reached the cave. We would have starved to death by now or been killed by the enemy at the border crossing,' June said.

Ron didn't reply. The lines in his face creased deeper.

'I am afraid of many things. One of them is the morale of our boys. You can see how anxious, depressed and silent they've become.' Then he spoke about a different matter. 'There are many villages near the border, even on this side, which I know well, and I know many people would help though, of course, we would have to make a hefty payment. I was even thinking of keeping the leader in one such house as it would be safe. The promise of more money to come would ensure the leader's safety for a couple of months. Then when the coast is clear, I could come back with a group and proper equipment and rapidly take him away from there. What do you say?'

'But can he stay in such a house alone? Even if we are able to take him there?'

'I am counting on you to stay with the leader.'

'No!' The word came out of June's mouth loudly. 'I will not be able to do it, sorry, no. Once near the border, I will be the first to attempt its crossing, come what may.'

Ron remained silent, then said in a low voice, 'We will cross that bridge when we come to it.'

Both of them remained silent for some time. June was angry. *How could he think that I would stay with a living corpse on this side of the border? It was unfair!* She was herself surprised at the vehemence of her thought. She felt a bitter fluid flooding her mouth and wanted to spit it out.

Sensing her anger, he tried to mollify her. 'Don't worry about that unnecessarily. It may not come to that. I was just thinking aloud of one of the possibilities. Look at the sky. Do you see it? To me, it is not a normal colour. Look at the pattern of light, how different it is. It does not bode well. I am really afraid that there may be early snow this year.'

June had to agree that Ron's words proved prophetic. Although in a different way.

The first change came in the sky.

When Ron had said that the sky looked abnormal, June couldn't make out much. The sky in these mountainous areas changed nearly every hour. Then slowly, she remembered the changes. The sky increasingly looked more and more opaque like ground glass and within a couple of days, the last traces of blue disappeared and the sky had become a dirty white, then grey and greyer still. She was then filled with a sense of foreboding.

Then one morning the wind rose. Steady at first, it soon increased in speed and force and along with it came a low cooing sound, which soon went on to become a high-pitched whining. By nightfall it became a horrendous howl. The cave door made from branches lashed together by ropes was in danger of being blown away many times. Two boys constantly tried to reinforce it with stouter branches. Though it could stop the wind to a great extent, there was no protection from the howling sound, which resounded with a screeching echo within the cave.

Till late in the morning next day, the wind continued to howl. It was nerve-wracking for everyone.

The wind subsided for a few hours, but then rose again

with still greater force. It raged for the next two days without let up.

~

During the gale, everybody had to stay inside the cave. First they tried to joke about it, saying it was wonderful that they did not have to go out for the bone-chilling sentry duty, of being able to lie down most of the time and stay idle. Soon, however, the jokes stopped and everyone became sombre and anxious. June watched with amusement how three groups had formed out of the nine inmates. The groups largely kept to themselves, talking among themselves and only June was the common member of the groups, moving from one to the other. Though nobody said so openly, the storm which raged outside was their main concern. They tried to recollect storms they had faced in the past but it was soon apparent that nobody had faced a storm more severe than the present one.

'We did have a big storm when we were building the camp,' Ron said. 'Do you remember that, sir?' he asked the leader.

The leader merely nodded, not adding anything.

He has become very silent since the beginning of the hailstorm, June thought. Most of the time he kept his eyes shut. Sometimes his lips moved silently as if he was praying or mumbling something.

She once asked him, 'Are you praying or saying something, sir?'

'Neither,' he had replied. 'I am meditating. I select a

word and meditate on it. It is called TM—transcendental meditation, you know? You can meditate on the word 'Om' or even on a pine cone. It brings great peace—you should also try it.'

'I will,' June said, 'but I don't know how to.'

'You only learn it by doing it. You start by making your mind blank.'

'My mind has already become blank, sir; there is nothing in it.'

Ron heard her speaking about her state of mind but did not comment.

28

THEN CAME THE snow, descending like a wet, white sheet.

It was such a sudden occurrence that everybody was caught unawares.

Though the high wind had ceased to blow, it was still strong enough to drive the snow through the open cave mouth when the door was opened.

Ron was the first to see the snow.

He got up early, at the crack of dawn as was his habit, and went to open the door. The sound of the wind had gone down and he anticipated a clear sky. *The storm has ceased*, he thought, *and the worst should be over*.

The boy on sentry duty inside the cave door had wrapped himself up with a rough, heavy rug into a cocoon and had gone to sleep sitting on the wooden block. Ron didn't wake him up. He removed the wooden branches placed as props in a slanting way to support the door against the wind and put them neatly on one side.

The cave was in total darkness. It was difficult to see the outlines of things inside although he could faintly make out the bed of the leader. The fire had long died down. The corner where June slept was very dark. A faint sound of snoring came from the depth of the dark cave. *That must be Kumbang*, thought Ron with amusement.

Through the gaps in the door, faint light filtered in from the outside. *Dawn has not yet broken fully*, Ron thought. Then he pulled one side of the door away, just enough to squeeze through, and stepped outside.

He stopped immediately, rubbed his eyes and looked up again. It felt as if the sky had come closing in up to the cave mouth! 'What the...!' he exclaimed softly. Then he muttered, 'Oh, it's snow falling! Snow, snow, my God! Everything has turned white! This is the last thing we needed...'

He crossed back carefully into the cave, keeping the door partially ajar so that light could come in. Then he went to the fireplace and built a small fire atop the warm ashes. Surprisingly, with the snowfall, the cold seemed to have decreased. He carefully built the small fire and went on adding small dry pieces of wood until there was a cheerful blaze inside. The flickering light from the flames started dancing inside his eyes. Rubbing them vigorously he filled water in the battered pot and placed it over the fire to boil.

He could make out that the cave was slowly stirring to life.

From the corner of his eyes, he saw June hurrying down towards the exit. As he expected, he soon heard her scream resonating in the cave and smiled.

The sentry woke up with a start and nearly fell off from the wooden block. Ron heard the excited voices of the boys near the back entrance and amidst that the high-pitched shrieks of June. He went near the leader and saw he was still sleeping. *Let him sleep*, Ron thought. *The storm had really affected and depressed him and the news of the snowfall may make him worry more.*

The snow fell for three days, at times very heavily. Then there was a one-day gap and then it started again, snowing continuously. And soon, there came a sense of resignation amongst the cave dwellers.

June herself was secretly elated, why she didn't know, but the snow brought her a secret happiness. She thought about it, tried to put a finger on the cause of her joy, but couldn't. *I shouldn't be happy when all the others are dejected,* she told herself. *I should meditate, as the leader had told me to. That will help me to banish these kinds of thoughts from my mind.*

She sat cross-legged on her bed and started with breathing exercises, pranayama. She started her meditation with the holy word 'Om', but after a while she discovered that she was thinking about something else, and soon her thoughts veered off to the wolves!

What are the poor wolves doing during the storms and snowfall? They must have their own caves somewhere in the mountains, just like us. They will only require small caves to protect them from the wind, rain and snow, where the cubs can huddle with their mother, curling up near her belly, getting the warmth from her body and trying desperately to feed. Will the male go out and howl during the snowfall? No, I don't think he will. How will they find food in the snow? Then she remembered that all creatures, big and small, who do not hibernate like bears during the winter do have to come out in search of food. Hares, rats and all others animals! And the wolves and other carnivores would hunt them when they came out. She was so completely lost in her reverie of the wolves that she had completely forgotten about the time. Only when Pradip came and nudged her, saying that the leader had been calling out for her for quite some time, did she came to her senses. She hurried to stoke the fire to a small cheerful blaze to warm up the broth she had cooked.

Pradip's reaction to the enforced confinement in the cave had been quite amusing. He had become a stickler for cleanliness. He would start in the morning, systematically sweeping the cave from one end to the other. His meticulous sweeping would be followed by scrubbing and wiping the area around the leader's bed, the fireplace and the entry point. He would try to wipe the wet places dry. Soon his zeal caught on and everybody lent a hand. The cave really shone as a result of their efforts. June observed that after a few days, the enthusiasm waned and ultimately, it was Pradip alone who religiously went on cleaning the cave.

Ron also had observed this, so when the boys stopped coming forward voluntarily, he joined Pradip in his cleaning drive. The leader also supported him, saying, 'We all are staying inside the cave now almost all the time. We are forced to do so by the elements. In this enforced period of inactivity we do not have much physical exercise, do we? The cleaning gives us physical activity; it energizes our limbs and improves the hygiene of our space…' He had rambled on for a long time and everybody listened silently, almost reverentially.

In the afternoon, though it was difficult to make out morning from afternoon inside the cave, the cave would become totally silent. June would sit near the half-open door and watch the sky and the white world outside where snow was falling softly. The leader would be sleeping. At the back of the cave, other cave inmates would either sleep, sit or quietly talk amongst themselves.

Ron came and sat near June on the cave floor on one such afternoon.

She turned her head and looked at him.

Ron started without any preamble, 'Now what should we do?'

'Do about what?'

Ron made a gesture of helplessness with his hands, 'How to avoid boredom? You know I have tried ludo and chess competitions, even the idiotic "antakshari". Ha, that was your bright idea! One boy had to sing a couplet of a song and when he stopped, another boy had to start with a song that begins with the last letter of the last couplet. Foolish!'

'Why are you venting your frustration on antakshari?'

'Maybe I am, but nothing seems to arouse the interest of our boys and the hilarious part is that they do not know enough songs to play the game. How does one entertain them?'

'Send them outside.'

'What?'

'Yes, they are not unfamiliar with snow. There used to be quite heavy snow in the camp also.'

'So?'

'Send them out, let them freeze to the bones in the cold outside, give them chores that will keep them busy. Put them on sentry duty. They are wild boys. It is a miracle that they have remained so peaceful, confined to the cave for such a long time, without murdering one another.'

The vehemence of June's words unsettled Ron.

'I will cut their rations to half…' June hissed. 'They only eat and sleep most of the time. You should go out and lead them. The boys are turning pale living inside the cave all the time.'

'What about you? Aren't you also in the same situation?'

'Don't try to needle me,' June said 'I will also go out. Try to take our leader out to the ledge if it snows lightly like now. We can wrap him in blankets.'

Ron appreciated June's words. The boys were basically outdoor creatures who thrived on outdoor work. There were some let ups between the hailstorm, gale and the snowfall for short periods so they could easily be sent outside. The leader opposed his plan as he was really afraid of mountain storms. The wind forces funnelled by the mountains could reach frightening proportions and actually lift up and sweep people off their feet. 'I have seen even mules blown away,' he said. He virtually ordered everybody to stay inside the cave and even outside sentry duty posts were brought inside the cave.

'The leader wants all of us around him during storms,' June started to say as if she could read Ron's thoughts. 'He told me that he would like to hear our voices. Staying together would keep the morale up, but we have seen that inactivity inside the cave has made the boys depressed. They have become dejected and silent, not knowing what to do. And most have lost their appetites too. Send them out as soon as possible. Why not now? It's snowing lightly...'

'I will,' Ron said. He then called three of the boys and told them to go out and bring some dried wood from the outside stock below the ledge. 'We have already burned one third of the stock inside—go out and replenish it.'

The boys who heard his orders immediately perked up, smiled, and got ready to go out.

'Just be careful,' Ron said, 'the ledge is slippery with the snow.'

June also went out to the ledge. The whole meadow below was white, only the big boulders showing black in the snowfield. The bushes and the pines were laden with snow on their leaves and branches. She thought that there may be a feet or more of snow in the meadow. She put out her hand and the snowflakes that fell on her palm melted immediately. The sky was dusky white. The outlines of the mountains could be barely made out.

Ron came out and joined her.

'It's really surprising for the early snowfall to be so heavy, about two feet of snow in the meadow. In the gullies it would be deeper. I think there the snow may be four feet deep.'

June turned and looked at him.

'All this snow is going to melt. It is not yet time for the main winter snowfall which will come a month or so later. And you know what will happen? All the snow melt will rush down though the gullies to the streams and go down to the rivers. And it would cause early floods in Assam...'

29

'I am a little disturbed by Sona's behaviour.' June broached the subject when both Ron and the leader were together. For the last few days it had been troubling her.

Sona was a strong boy, tall and well built, with a plain face that seemed to clearly proclaim that he was from a village, a country boy. There was a scar above his right eyebrow. He was a very reliable stretcher-bearer. He was not a talker, and spoke only when he was spoken to. Though a little withdrawn, there was no reason to think that he was abnormal. But with the continuous inclement weather of the last few days, he had become more and more withdrawn. With the snowfall, he started behaving oddly. He would sit alone, hardly ever talking to the other boys. When spoken to he would reply in monosyllables, sometimes not at all.

June was mostly disturbed by the vacant staring look that came to his face when he was alone. 'He is very anxious and depressed, but what disturbs me most is his uncommunicative state,' June voiced her worries before Ron and the leader.

Ron said, 'Each person is different from others. Don't

you know the saying, "There is a germ in every grain of paddy and a mind in every person."? Some worry more than others, what can you do? With a little more time he will be all right; like the other boys he will be resigned to his fate.'

The leader was silent and had closed his eyes. Ron's eyes had a slight glint of impatience.

'He has a restless aura. You can easily make out that. He is possibly worried about going back.'

'Aren't we all?'

'Yes, but accepting the inevitability of fate is something that doesn't come easily to everyone.'

'What can you do? It can't be helped.'

Why is Ron shying away from doing something? In fact, he is refusing to even acknowledge the problem! June thought. Then she realized it was probably not kind to talk about the inevitability of fate before the leader, since he was ensnared by his destiny, his paralysis. So even though she wanted to continue the conversation, she stopped. At that moment she saw Kumbang smiling like a fool from a distance. She became angry with him. Lately, he had attached himself to Ron, following him everywhere like a puppy, thinking he had a special relationship with Ron after his journey with him down to the valley. June had tried to convey her displeasure with a sneer or two, but he ignored her. She shouted at him, 'Why don't you go out of the cave with your sling? All the hares and rodents are coming out of their lairs into the snow-covered fields. Go and hunt some.'

Kumbang was taken aback by her sharp tone. He

immediately turned around, picked up his sling and pellets from his bed roll and rushed down towards the rear exit.

When June saw Ron smiling at her outburst, she was doubly annoyed. She rose and stomped out of the cave through the front entrance, leaving the two bemused leaders behind.

June saw Pradip standing below the ledge and throwing pieces of firewood into it from the stockpile below. The wood stock was also covered by a mantle of snow and the height from the ledge to the ground below had decreased considerably due to the accumulated snow.

June greeted Pradip from above and then hurried down the footholds on the edge of the ledge. When she reached, she could feel the soft snow below, the feeling of her feet sinking into the snow giving her a pleasurable thrill. Suddenly, she sank in the snow up to her knees. She gave a squeal of delight, but Pradip looked concerned. 'Hey, don't move!' he shouted. 'The snow is quite deep.'

June tried to dig in her feet in the snow below, but she sank another six inches or so.

Pradip called out in alarm, 'Hey, look out! The snow there may be deeper.'

'It is,' June said 'I feel I am constantly sinking down. And I don't think I can get out myself.'

'Wait, I am coming,' Pradip said, stepping gingerly in the soft snow.

He extended his hand but June didn't immediately grasp it. She made him take one more step and when he did so, she caught hold of his hand and pulled him towards her.

Pradip nearly stumbled in the soft snow. June then put her arms around his neck and said, 'Pull me up.'

Pradip tried, but it was not easy to pull her up from knee-deep snow. In the process, June placed her face on Pradip's bare neck and embraced him. Her lips touched his warm skin and the smell of his body filled her nostrils and imagination, a pleasurable warmth spreading throughout her body. She didn't remove her face and lips from Pradip's neck. Pradip heaved with all his might, tightly embracing June below her arms. June felt her breasts pressing against his chest. In the pulling and heaving that ensued, both of them got out from the snow but tumbled together into it again.

Pradip got up and looked at June.

She was still lying on the snow, but Pradip didn't extend his hand to pick her up. June saw that his eyes were shining with a strange gleam. June slowly looked away, still remembering his raw, intoxicating smell. She closed her eyes. Then she slowly got up from the snow and went towards the wood pile.

'I think you have collected enough wood for today. Don't gather any more, otherwise it crowds the ledge and the cave,' June told a silent Pradip, who was still looking at her. 'Let us climb up to the ledge. The big pieces shall have to be made into small splinters so that the fire does not get smoky.'

She then went towards the steps and climbed up nimbly like a mountain goat. Pradip followed her without speaking.

From the ledge, June looked at the wide expanse of snow dotted by boulders. She suddenly saw a crouching figure in the distance! She wondered who it was. The figure was crouching near a boulder. *I should have brought binoculars*, she told herself. *That must be Kumbang. What is he doing there? Is he really hunting hares? My God, I shouldn't have asked him to go out like that. Ron could have stopped him. That headstrong boy will not come back without bringing something. How to call him? Since the wind is blowing from that side, he won't hear me even if I shout.*

Then she saw Sona sitting alone on the narrow end of the ledge. Gesturing to Pradip that she would be back soon, she hurried along the uneven ledge towards Sona.

She went and sat near him.

He didn't look at her but stared vacantly towards the whiteness before him.

After some time June started tentatively, 'What is the matter, Sona? You always look so worried.'

He didn't reply.

'We all are very anxious. This weather was totally unexpected.'

'Already such deep snow,' Sona somehow mumbled.

'The snow is untimely. It was expected only after a month or so. Ron sir says it will melt and the water will go down towards Assam, causing early floods.'

He didn't reply.

'Have you experienced snow before?'

He nodded slightly.

'With the snowfall, the cold actually decreases. It's the wind before the snow which brings in the cold.'

Sona didn't reply. So June tried a different way to get through to him.

'Sona, we all are really worried. This is a very unexpected situation. We are a group of only nine people facing a difficult time so we must stay united, stick to each other…'

Sona didn't reply but maintained a moody silence. After some time, he suddenly said, 'I will die if I have to stay the winter here.' Then with a heavy sigh, Sona rose and leaving June behind, went off with a hunched gait and climbed down from the ledge.

Towards evening, the wind rose again.

It came with a cooing sound which was quite peculiar and unlike any other sound they had heard before. There was moonlight but flaky clouds rushed into the ashen white sky, casting shadows creating eerie patterns on the white expanse below. The rising wind brought a bone-chilling cold too.

June caught hold of Kumbang and pulled him outside. 'Come outside. I have something important to say to you.'

'I don't want to go out into the windy cold. We can sit near the fire and you can tell me there.'

'No, it's so beautiful outside, what with the moonlight, clouds and snow. Don't you like it?'

'I don't like the cold.'

'What I want to talk to you about is Sona.' June paused for a while. 'He is so depressed, I am worried about him. We all have to stay together through thick and thin, don't we?'

Kumbang didn't respond.

'We have to do something, don't we?'

'What?'

'Keep him company, stay near him, try to make him worry less.'

'I can't do it.'

'Why?'

'He stinks!'

'What? What does he stink of?'

'He smells of decay, of death.'

'What…what are you saying?'

'Yes, didn't you get the smell?'

'Stop talking rubbish. If you don't want to help him, don't, but don't say such weird things about him. We should try to help if we can. Don't forget that by helping him we are also helping ourselves.'

Their conversation ceased and both of them watched the ever-changing sky and the dance of shadows on the snow below. June placed her arm over his shoulders and held him close to her like a friend.

'Hear the sound of the wind. Doesn't it sound like a woman wailing?'

Kumbang cocked his ears as if trying to hear it better. 'It is still faint,' he said. 'If the wind increases it may become louder.'

'I wonder what the wolves are doing.'

'Wolves?'

'The wolf pack that lives around these mountains. I feel that they are our wolves like the jackal pack in our village which I also feel to be my very own pack.'

'They must be feeling cold and must be staying within their lairs, all curled up.'

'Yes, think about the cubs.'

'Cubs? How do you know they have cubs?'

'I don't know, but what's the harm in imagining that they have cubs. Haven't you heard the wolves howling?'

'Heard them many times and when we went down to the valley, one howled quite nearby.'

'Will you be able to howl like them?'

'Yes, I can. I can perfectly imitate all voices.'

'Can you? Why don't you let out a howl.'

'Should I?'

'Yes, do it. I will join you.'

Kumbang cupped his hands in front of his month, and first let out a low throaty howl, and then a long wailing one.

June tried to join him, but couldn't do it as perfectly as Kumbang. She soon gave up and started laughing.

After howling a few times. Kumbang stopped and tried to hear if there was any response from the real wolves. There was none, only the rising wind moaned softly.

'You must have been a wolf in one of your previous lives,' June said.

Kumbang gave her his idiotic smile, caught hold of June's hand and pulled her towards the cave door. 'Come, let's go inside, it's getting colder.'

30

WHEN THE WIND rises in the mountains, everything else stops.

Someone from the villages near the camp had told this to Ron long ago. Now he told June. She pricked up her ears. Even inside the cave, the wailing howl of the wind could be heard. What had happened again? The storm, snowfall, everything had stopped. Though the sky was mostly overcast, there was no other change. The wind blew, but it was not very strong, not a storm. The only peculiarity she noticed this time was that the wind made a cooing, moaning sound which was new. Now when the wind rose in the late afternoon, it lashed everything. It came in great gusts and then would die down, only to return again. It had even scattered the snow from different places. The wind seemed to lift the snow from the open flat areas and drive it towards the gullies and the mountainside where it accumulated. Soon the wind became so snow-laden that it became nearly opaque. When the wind went down for some time and the cave inmates could come out to the ledge, they could see large bare patches in the meadow from where the snow had been driven by the wind. It had formed large mounds. June could see that the wind was constantly sculpting the snowscape.

She, Pradip, Kumbang and Ron, all stayed out in the ledge till it became dark. Then the wind became stronger and the chill froze them to the marrow. Without exchanging a word, as if on a cue, they trooped into the cave and towards the fireplace.

The leader was on his bed. He was awake. When they entered, he smiled faintly and said, 'What did you see outside? From the sound of the wind, I feel a blizzard is coming.'

'A blizzard?' June asked.

'Yes, a violent snow storm. And that would be the end of the bad weather. The amount of snow that can fall in this early winter will fall tonight and then the weather will improve.'

'Are you sure?'

'I have been told it happens like that. Either it starts by a blizzard or ends by one.'

'I hope that is true.'

'I think it is true. I have been told by people who know these things. This blizzard will be the last one and then the weather will lift. Sunshine will melt the powdery snow and ice will form. Mark my words.'

Ron sat near the leader. June and Pradip also came near and sat down. Kumbang stoked the fire, building it into a cheerful blaze. Pradip then asked tentatively, 'Will that open up ways to move out from here?'

'That depends. Two things are likely to happen. The gullies that we have to cross will be covered by snow and ice. Down below, that is below the snowline, the gullies, nullahs and streams will be full of rushing water from the snowmelt. It will not be easy to cross both of them, that much I can tell you.'

'We will then have to pass the winter here,' Pradip said.

The leader pursed his lips but didn't say anything.

Ron interjected a little impatiently. 'Pradip, we must be ready for any eventuality. I don't think going down early is a good option. After the attack on the camp and the dispersal of our forces, the police and the spies must be keeping a close watch on the border and all travel points. And we don't know the condition of our organization in the valley. We have been cut off from everyone. It will not be easy to re-establish contact…' Ron paused. Pradip nodded wordlessly.

And even if some contact is made, it will be very difficult to trust anyone, June thought.

'And don't forget,' Ron said, 'our first duty is to preserve our leader and take him down to Assam safely.'

All of them nodded vigorously.

June saw that the leader was mumbling 'thank you' but had closed his eyes.

She felt a little uneasy and wanted this kind of talk to stop. So she declared, 'I will cook khichidi today and try to make a dish of fried potatoes, but I don't know how it'll taste. The potatoes have really shrunk and have become sweet and I have only forty dry chillies left for some taste.'

'You have counted them?' Pradip asked and laughed.

'You have to count everything,' she said and added, 'Don't laugh, the days are not far off when all you will get is some rice and salt.'

'If you could, you would do that even now.'

June gave him a severe look.

'I have an idea,' Ron said. 'What if we roast the potatoes inside the hot ashes and embers in the fireplace? They may turn out to be tasty.'

'Master stroke!' the leader suddenly said, approving of the idea.

Kumbang immediately jumped up to fetch the potatoes.

'Don't you touch my stores!' June shouted and immediately followed him. Everybody laughed heartily.

By the time they finished dinner, the blizzard was in full blast. The wind roared, howled and shrieked, and periodically banged and shook the cave door, threatening to blow it away. The whole cave became silent. Nobody spoke. Ron and Pradip tried to tend to the front door while two boys went to the rear door. The leader lay in his bed, still like a flat piece of timber. June sat on her bed and observed everyone. Despite the doors, gusts of wind blew in through the gaps in the planks, driving snow inside. The fire nearly went out, the flames flattened by incoming air blasts. Kumbang tried to keep a small fire burning in the hearth for light but it was not easy. The fire threw only a reddish glow in the front part of the cave, making it impossible to see anything with clarity.

It was as if a thousand witches were wailing outside, sweeping around the ledge like big birds of prey. And inside the cave, the sound and its echoes reverberated and knocked repeatedly at the walls, creating a continuous and disturbing vibration. June clamped her hands tightly over her ears and closed her eyes. It did shut out the sounds and the disturbance, but would immediately assail the senses the moment she removed her hands. Suddenly, June felt as if someone was standing near her. Even with her eyes closed she could feel the presence. She became afraid, a chill running down her spine. Then, unable to resist her curiosity, she slowly opened her eyes. At first she didn't see anything. Then things came into focus slowly. Kumbang was kneeling near the fire, tending it. A red glow had spread inside the front part of the cave. And near the low barrier of rice sacks and boxes stood a shadow.

'Who? Who is it? June asked.

Then the shadow spoke, 'I am hungry, give me something to eat.'

Sona…it was Sona!

Didn't he eat tonight, before the main blizzard, when gruel was cooked? She distinctly remembered Sona eating his portion silently along with the mashed roasted potatoes.

She sat up. Nobody in the cave had ever asked for food like this. What should she give him? She was at a loss.

'I can give you some chira. I will soften it with water and will give you some sugar. Will that do?'

The shadow nodded.

June got up. She placed some flaked rice in an aluminium dish, poured some warm water from the kettle and stirred it. The flaked rice soon absorbed the water, swelled and became soft. Then she liberally sprinkled the dish with sugar and gave it to Sona. He took the dish from June, sat down on his haunches and started to eat.

Kumbang looked at her quizzically from near the fire, but she ignored him.

The outline of the leader's cot could be made out faintly in the darkness but he couldn't be seen.

Ron was also nowhere to be seen.

Where had he gone? She looked towards the area where he slept and could see the outline of a person curled up there, asleep. He would get up soon and relieve Kumbang.

She thought it would be nice to be able to sleep curled up with Kumbang, stretching a hand across his chest, burying her nose into the smooth skin at the nape of his neck. More like a brother than a lover... She so much liked the idea that she, too, curled up in the bed, imagining Kumbang beside her, even though a little ashamed for thinking in that way.

While the blizzard raged outside, she fell into a deep sleep.

When she woke up in the morning, she was disoriented for some time. There was pin-drop silence and she wondered why. She sat up quickly. Then she remembered the blizzard and its furious sounds. Now there was no sound, which meant the blizzard had blown away. Light was filtering through the gaps in the door.

As she stood up, she saw Kumbang sleeping wrapped up in his heavy prickly rug near the fireplace, right where he had been sitting at night. Why? Didn't Ron relieve him at night? She looked towards Ron's bed and could see his curled up figure. Sympathetically, she thought he must have slept through, must have been too tired, the poor man. Kumbang must not have woken him up at the appointed time and was sure to get a dressing down today for not doing so.

June got up, put on her layers of tattered socks and got her feet into her misshapen shoes. Then she went to the door to remove the props, but somehow they were stuck tight and she had to use as much force as she could to get them away. After removing the props, she tried to open the door. The moment she opened it, something heavy pushed the door in and a large chunk of something broke and fell inside the cave, making her scream.

It was a large chunk of snow, as big as a quintal sack.

It fell inside the cave and broke into a heap right at her feet.

As she looked at it in horror, she screamed again.

Kumbang and Ron shook themselves awake and ran towards her hurriedly.

Their eyes were red and swollen.

Within a moment, Ron could make out what had happened. He laughed out loudly.

'A little more and we would have been trapped and buried inside the cave.'

June looked at the mass of snow at her feet and started crying.

Ron and Kumbang tried to calm her, saying, 'Don't cry, don't cry.'

'Look we are still alive,' Ron said, 'and the storm has blown away.'

All the other boys who were inside the cave crowded

around the door. Ron left her and went to the leader who had called out to him.

Somehow June couldn't control her crying, her shoulders heaving with silent sobs. She could feel Kumbang embracing her tightly.

They didn't have shovels. The boys took the long logs used as props for the door and tried to push away the snow from the door. The rear door also had to the cleared. The blizzard, which carried the snow after hitting the face of the mountain, had deposited it over all over ledge, back passage and at the foot of the mountain, in high, thick piles.

When June came to light the fire at the hearth, Ron requested, 'Please make sweet black tea today.'

They didn't have many tea leaves to start with—only one large plastic container full of mouldy tea leaves. So, when it was half gone, June had stopped giving tea to anyone, except the leader.

On this day, she made tea for everyone with lots of sugar (which she had stopped using long back) and gave a large mugful to everyone.

As they sipped the hot sweet tea rapturously, Pradip, who had gulped his mugful down and had begun to clean the cave, said in a worried voice, 'Sona is nowhere to be seen!'

The news exploded like an electric flash inside the cave.

'What do you mean Sona is nowhere to be seen?' Ron asked sharply.

'Can't find him anywhere' Pradip said. 'I looked around and went to look at the toilet, which is half under snow. He is not there or anywhere.'

'When did anybody see him last?'

June told them in a trembling voice how strangely he had come to ask for food at night, saying he was hungry and how she had fed him flaked rice with sugar.

Kumbang nodded. He had seen that.

'The blizzard was going on at full force then,' they added.

Ron immediately rushed out from the rear with Pradip and the boys, indicating to Kumbang to stay back with the leader and June.

Both of them went and sat near the leader. He was also very disturbed. Anxiety, even fear, was writ large on his face.

'Mountain blizzards are like witches,' he said in a low voice, 'they entice and snatch away people. I have heard such stories. Now I have seen them come true.'

June started crying again. The leader did not say anything. Neither did Kumbang, but he placed his hand softly on her back.

'All the mountain witches come out from their lairs during storms. They dance with the gusts of air, slide, glide, turn over, somersault and play in the winds. The more fierce the storm, the happier they are. It is they who break the trees, sometimes uproot them, kill the birds, break their nests...' the leader went on saying.

'Who told you this, sir?' Kumbang asked. 'Many tribal people believe in such stories, specially the hill tribes.'

The leader didn't answer directly. He went on, 'When the malevolent witches are out, they look for blood, both human and animal....'

June sobbed loudly. Kumbang patted her consolingly.

She said, 'He must have been really depressed. I had no way of knowing. He seldom came to me and never to ask for food. He must have been really depressed to have walked out into the blizzard like that to sure death, suicidal death.'

31

THEY HAD SEARCHED far and wide for Sona but found no trace of him. He had just disappeared into thin air. He couldn't have travelled far in the blizzard so Ron said they were sure to find him, but they didn't.

June and Kumbang also went out to search for him. Ron had allocated different areas for pairs to search.

'Did the blizzard carry him away?' June had asked.

'The witches, the witches that came out during the storm, the witches that whistled and moaned with the wind must have carried him away. Must have lifted him and crushed him against the mountains.'

'Don't say that.'

'He may have been thrown into a crevice.'

'We have searched most of them,' June said, and then added, 'By any chance, could he still be alive?'

'Most unlikely. His body must be lying under the heaps of snow and…'

'And what?'

'The wolves must have eaten up his body.'

'What?' June nearly screamed. Then she started shivering and her teeth chattered. With a great effort she controlled herself and whispered, 'Kumbang! Are you sure?'

'It looks like it. Otherwise, how could he disappear like this? In that gale and in that darkness he couldn't have gone far. He must have lost consciousness and frozen to death. We have looked for him everywhere but couldn't find his body.'

'It stands to reason that after his death, the wolves must have devoured him. Don't you remember, how the wolves had howled madly after the blizzard?'

June remembered that and she shivered again.

'But if it was so,' she said slowly, 'what happened to his clothes? We should have found those clothes.'

'When the wolves mauled the body, they must have torn the clothes to shreds. They must have got dirtied and discoloured and the wind must have scattered the shreds to God knows where. And the wolves can break any bones and chew them to bits…'

June's eyes brimmed over. Kumbang said, 'You know, they can even drag the body over a long distance and hide the remains in some inaccessible crag.'

Then he turned towards June and said, 'June baideu, please don't cry. This is only one of the possibilities. It might not have been like that at all.'

June knew he was trying to console her, comfort her. Her intuition told her that it was the most possible scenario, that this was what must have happened. But she didn't want to acknowledge it or believe it.

She patted Kumbang on the back and said, 'Let us go back to our cave…'

The sun shone nearly for a fortnight.

During the morning hours, it could be as strong as in summer. The snow melted fast. Dirty ice formed in some creeks, then started melting, giving rise to trickles of water. In the afternoon, the cold would start with a light breeze blowing from the mountains and within hours it would be chilly.

Winter is coming, thought June, *this time it's really coming*. She sniffed the air as if trying to detect the smell of the approaching winter.

'Thinking about the coming winter, aren't you?' said Pradip, who was standing on the ledge with June and Kumbang. June looked at him vacantly, in an absent-minded way.

Ron joined them at that moment. 'The winter will set in soon,' he said as if he could gauge their thoughts. 'We now have to discuss the situation very seriously.'

June sat down on the ledge with her back to the stone face of the mountain. She couldn't help thinking worriedly about how Ron could possibly be raising this topic now, with the leader still in such bad shape. It didn't escape Ron's notice.

'Can we think of moving now, with the leader so sick?' she asked, more to herself than to the others, her concern weighing on her heart heavily. Her tone was such that it didn't call for any reply.

'It is most important that we discuss the whole matter more seriously now,' Pradip and Kumbang nodded solemnly. June was distressed. She looked into the distance where the sky was turning fast into a sheet of glass and the mountains into glass etchings.

After the blizzard was over, the leader was struck by fever and soon a dry, hacking cough started. They had all discussed the matter amongst themselves, bringing out the medicine store they had with them. They could identify some antibiotic capsules and paracetamol tablets, with which they started the treatment of the leader. There was no medicine for the cough—they had nothing better to offer except hot water and tea made out of the mouldy leaves. Ron discovered a half-empty small tin of Vicks balm in his knapsack. June used it on the leader and smeared a little of it on his forehead and nostrils, after which he would sleep fitfully.

The leader tried to cooperate fully with the treatment. Only June saw his frightened eyes from time to time, his efforts to look unconcerned were rather pathetic. Her heart twisted in sadness in those moments.

In desperation, she started singing lullabies to him. That soon became a pattern. He would ask her to sing this or that, mainly old melodies. June herself was surprised that she remembered most of them, both lyrics and tunes, and would sing in a low voice as if humming to herself.

'I never knew you could sing so well,' Ron once remarked.

'I myself didn't know it,' June replied.

The leader apparently didn't like to share her singing with anyone, even Ron and Kumbang. He made it clear in many subtle ways. The hint was taken by both Ron and Kumbang, who then left her alone with the leader for the singing sessions.

Ron didn't say anything about it but the irrepressible Kumbang had to comment, 'So you sing only for the leader, do you?'

'Why grudge him this little pleasure? You shouldn't,' June said pleasantly. 'I like to sing for him. At least there is somebody who appreciates my talent.'

Kumbang made a face at her.

⁓

Sitting on the ledge in the chilly afternoon and hearing Ron, Pradip and Kumbang discussing various possibilities, she wanted to cry. *What is happening to me?* June thought. *I am becoming too emotional.* She remembered the look of helplessness and fear on the face of the leader. The cough had caused back pain as well and shooting pains down his legs. There were lots of painkiller tablets in the medicine box which she recognized. She had to give him painkillers more frequently now. Worried, she became absent-minded and lost the thread of discussion between Ron and the others.

Then she heard Ron saying in a firm voice. 'We must make a realistic assessment now. If we move now, in this weather, will he be able to survive the ordeal?'

June became attentive.

'It is likely to take five to six days, maybe more, one never knows how events will turn…' Pradip said, but didn't complete the sentence.

June wanted to take an active part in the discussion. She felt that a decision was going to be taken so she didn't want to stay outside. She rose and stood near Ron, feeling immediately the relief of the others that she had come forward to take part in the discussion.

'It is really uncertain, but six days is a reasonable guess,' Ron said. 'He would be totally exposed to the elements. There can be snowfall, but once we can go down from the heights below the snowline, then snow won't be a problem any more. However, you can't totally discount occasional winter drizzles.'

'And all that time he will be totally exposed,' Kumbang said. 'He has a bad cough now, though it is getting a little better.'

'It is, but he is very sick. He still has a little fever from time to time,' June said.

Everybody looked towards Ron. He said, 'I would want individual opinions from all three of you. But before that let me put up another point. Do you clearly remember the way we had taken to reach this cave? Do you think there were areas which may now hold deep snow or ice, or with the snowmelt, do you think there may be areas where there would be water, swift currents that might be impassable?'

All of them tried to recall the gullies, the depressions, the valleys, the areas that looked like stony stream beds. Ron observed that Kumbang's memory was very sharp. So graphic were his descriptions of the path that it seemed like a video tape being played in reverse. Pradip and June filled in the details. They huddled on the ledge, very close together, and talked in hushed animated tones.

Their discussions continued as they remained oblivious to the cold.

June suddenly realized that in the entire discussion Ron had not said anything definite. He had not revealed his own thoughts or preferences.

She was perplexed at first, then she understood that he wanted the others to spell out what he must have been thinking himself. She was sure that Ron had already taken the decision not to move, not to risk taking out the sick leader in uncertain weather and over uncertain terrain.

Yes, he has already decided to spend the winter in the cave! That would mean nearly four or five more months in the cave! Four or five months more! June shuddered involuntarily at the very thought.

Would the leader last though the long winter?

June didn't want to think about it, but couldn't banish such thoughts from her mind altogether.

Ron is taking a very calculated risk, June thought. *To move immediately would be the most logical thing to do, but the leader would surely not make it in his condition.*

Either Ron was calculating on the leader remaining stable till the end of the winter or dying before that, in the cave. Then the rest of the group would be able to move swiftly and would have a better chance of making it alive to Assam, even in the winter.

It snowed softly.

Though the snowfall lasted only an hour or so, the whole world around the cave, the rock-strewn meadow, the shrubs and also the tall branches of the pine and deodars were covered with a light and fragile mantle of snow. The surroundings looked clean, white and delicately fragile.

June saw the snow falling through the open cave mouth. She looked with certain fascination. She was cooking the gruel for the leader and had put two potatoes under the hot ashes of the hearth. This was a treat the leader loved, slightly burned, roasted and mashed potato along with his gruel. Before the fever, the leader could eat by himself with the wooden spoon Kumbang had carved for him. In the reclining position, he could use the spoon to pick and put the gruel in his mouth. The day he could finish the plate himself, he would be very happy. But after the fever, he had not been able to do it. June thought once or twice to ask him to try eating again, then she thought better of it and refrained. *Asking him to try would put mental pressure on him*, she thought.

'Is it snowing again?' the leader had asked while he was being fed. From his bed he could also see the open cave mouth clearly.

'It looks like a light snow,' June said.

'Light snow is the real harbinger of winter,' he said. After a few moments he asked, 'I could make out that you are actively discussing about leaving the cave and going down. Though none of you have told me anything, I could sense it in my bones. If there was not that untimely storm and heavy snowfall, this would have been the right time to make the move. Do you know, Kumbang had already shown me a drawing of a light-weight stretcher carrier he has designed?'

'He is cutting various sized pieces from bamboo and wood. He won't say what he is doing with those,' June said.

'Ha, ha, those are for the stretcher. It will be light and strong and will also have a foldable structure above that can be covered with a plastic sheet. A real talented chap that guy is.'

'There is still time to make a move, don't you think? Once we can travel below the snowline…' the leader asked tentatively.

'We have to wait till you are completely well. Though your fever has come down, I think it is still there. It has not yet completely disappeared. But more important is your cough, which has to go. And you have become quite weak in these two weeks of fever and coughing. You have to regain your strength before we can make a move.'

'Are you thinking of staying the winter here?'

His voice was hesitant, as if he was a little afraid.

'Ron sir has not said anything definite yet. I think you are the first person he would talk to and discuss any plan with. I am sure. But the option of staying here for the winter was one possibility we had kept in mind from the day we had come to the cave, isn't it?'

'I know,' the leader said with a long sigh. Then he closed his eyes. June could make out that he had not gone to sleep and wanted to stay alone for some time. She rose and silently came out to the cave mouth. It was still snowing outside, light fluffy snowflakes were coming down from the sky in slow motion. She saw Ron sitting alone on the ledge, deep in thought.

She went in and brought out his breakfast, thick unleavened bread with a little sugar and a cup of steaming hot water in which she had added a few tea leaves. She also brought out her own mug and half a piece of bread. When she gave it to Ron, he accepted the breakfast gratefully and sipped the brew with apparent relish.

'So, have you taken a final decision?' she asked him in a soft, warm voice that had an immediate relaxing effect on Ron. He put a piece of bread into his month, took a long sip from the cup and turned to June.

'I am not yet able to take a final decision. Apart from the four of us who had discussed this matter, we have not talked it out with the other three. I am not sure what their reaction would be. Really, I am not sure. What if they want to go down on their own—it would create a very peculiar situation.'

June had not thought about that possibility.

'And what if Pradip or Kumbang want to go down with them? This is the right time and everybody knows it too. I am not even remotely implying that Pradip or Kumbang will do it, they are too disciplined for that. But can I be sure of you? What if you, too, want to go down?'

June looked up sharply at Ron. Then she saw that he was smiling, one of those very rare occasions when he had smiled spontaneously in a relaxed way. The smile had dissolved the studied sternness of his face along with its worry lines and seemed to lessen his age by a couple of years. June also smiled and said, 'I would really love to go… but all of us should go together.'

Ron nodded, then said contemplatively, 'Will we be able to do so?'

They went into an animated discussion, revisiting all the arguments, all the pros and cons they had discussed earlier. And soon both of them realized that they were moving within the same circle, moving again and again through the same path. They realized it wouldn't end by itself unless a firm decision was made.

'Now you have to take the decision, sir,' June said a little formally. 'Unless you take the decision, nothing is going to happen.'

Ron became silent. Then he said in a choked voice, 'You have to help me, June. I am finding it very difficult to take a decision. Let us talk about something we have not discussed before. I feel, I strongly feel, that as a soldier my first duty is to the commander. I can't leave the leader, neither can I expose him to risks which may harm him, on may even kill him. We all know he is not fit enough to travel at the moment. That he will improve with time, that possibility is also slim…' Ron stopped midway as if waiting for his breath to return.

June felt a wave of tenderness sweeping over her. She wanted to comfort Ron. She said in a low voice, 'He has borne his recent sickness very well. He has almost recovered! Don't you think so? The fever has almost gone down, the bouts of coughing are also decreasing. He is on the mend. The winter would be tough, but he may get through it fine. Also, should he deteriorate suddenly, unexpectedly and even die, we have to accept it.'

'Whatever it is, I will have to look after him till the end. Until I can place him in a safe place, that's my duty, my obligation. Do you think I am wrong?'

'No, you are absolutely right.'

'You think so? Really?'

'Yes, I think, under the circumstances, you are right.'

'Thank you, thank you. You have taken a load off my heart.'

June touched Ron's wrist and gave it a slight squeeze.

Ron was very pleasantly surprised. His face brightened, 'So we stay?' he asked.

'Yes, we stay, but…'

'But what?'

'Your decision should not be seen by others as a helpless surrender to the inevitable, to fate. It must be gradual. Ask Kumbang to construct the light stretcher with its foldable cover. Ask Pradip to make general preparations, ask me to prepare a food stock report. Put the other boys to work. With time they would all realize that the best way would be to stay the winter here.'

Ron looked at her in genuine surprise. 'You are right June, you are absolutely right,' he said with real warmth.

32

It was a bombshell that didn't shatter the cave inmates, tear them to pieces or kill them. It simply numbed them, totally numbed and paralysed them.

And it burst in the early morning.

They were all sleeping. Ron was curled up near the door, the leader in his high bed, June in her secluded alcove and Kumbang near the fireplace. He had shifted his lair from the allotted grass bed which he used to share with others to a place near the fire which remained warm. There he would put a folded rug and lie wrapped in another rug like a cat. 'Yes, a smelly tom cat,' June would tease him.

'I can't take off my clothes to wash them, it's too cold,' he would reply.

'Take them off, I'll wash them for you,' she would say and he would only laugh, his mischievous laugh with its little tinkle, which June liked very much.

Pradip came in and hissed, 'All of you—get up fast!' He pushed Kumbang roughly, came near June and said the same thing. Then he rushed to Ron, who was already stirring, and stood at attention.

Ron immediately got up. 'What is it, Pradip?'

'Sir, two of our boys are missing—Amlan and Pran, with their arms.'

June could hear Kumbang gasp.

'Were they on night duty?'

'Yes, sir.'

'All of you, come here!' commanded the leader from his bed.

They trooped towards his bed and stood in a line before him.

June felt totally dazed. The leader questioned Pradip closely. His voice was level and crisp. Both Pradip and Ron tried to answer his queries, while June listened silently, her mind blank and senses numb. She could gather that Amlan and Pran were on night duty together. Nobody knew when they had left. They had taken away two good weapons, an AK 47 and an SLR. Pradip wanted to immediately go in hot pursuit but the leader stopped him.

'Don't be a fool, Pradip,' he said. 'They have a four- to six-hour headstart over you. This is the bright phase of the moon and they must have travelled in the moonlight. If they have not travelled far and see you following, they may shoot you. Why, they could have shot and killed us all—we are lucky to be alive, you know! Deserters are ruthless.'

A quick search revealed that they had been able to take away large amounts of flaked rice, some implements, clothes and blankets.

'They have probably been planning this for quite a long time.'

June tried to think about when they could have taken

the food away from her store. Definitely, they had done it during the daytime when people were mostly outside the cave.

June thought, *What should I do now?* She went to the cave mouth and looked outside. Then she went to the ledge and gazed at the distance. The powdery snow had long melted. *What am I looking for? The fugitives or their footprints?* She looked long and hard towards the horizon, the distant clumps of trees in the forest, the boulders, the unhappy-looking sky and the indifferent mountain ranges. What did she expect to see? She felt a numbing blankness enveloping her and a sense of unexplained betrayal came over her. Why did Amlan and Pran decide to desert? They had never grumbled about anything, never said anything about going. They were not depressed like Sona was. She felt so drained that she didn't want to think about it any more.

~

'Do you know what the punishment for desertion is? Death. It is death.'

The leader and Ron had called all of them together to a conclave near the leader's bed. They silently gathered. Nobody had had breakfast that day, there was no cooking. At Ron's orders, Kumbang made strong tea for them and June gave everyone biscuits from their dwindling stock. She had kept some packets separately in a plastic jar, thinking that they would be useful for the return journey. The deserters had not been able to take biscuits from her stock.

They sat huddled near the leader and he spoke.

'I will tell you a story—something that happened long ago. Ron must have heard about it. At that time, too, we were outside India, in the Kachin country in upper Burma. We had a few hundred cadres in our camps and we lived there with the support of the Kachin independent army and our Naga brothers. It was never an easy time. Apart from the food scarcity, there was fighting and we helped our Naga and Kachin brothers in their battles with the savage Burmese army. It was like an ordeal by fire for our boys, a first-hand experience of actual war. We had casualties, but we accepted that. But the greatest danger was the threat of unknown diseases, some caused by poisonous insect bites. And these could mean death, you know. At the time there was rumour of a large-scale attack by the Burmese army, causing immense worry, anxiety and even fear amongst the new recruits—that I won't deny.

'And once two of the new recruits deserted camp. They ran away to the forest and hills. In those places they wouldn't have survived anyhow, the paths being unknown to them in that inhospitable terrain. But our boys went in hot pursuit. We sent messages to our friends also by wireless—and it was they who caught the two deserters.'

'The deserters were caught?' June asked in a tremulous voice.

'Yes, and handed back to us.'

'Then what happened?'

'It was decided to make an example out of them.'

'Example? What did you decide to do to the two young boys…?' June's voice broke.

The leader ignored her all together. He went on as if he had not heard her at all. 'The leadership decided to give them the death penalty for desertion and make it such a spectacle that it may appear to all of you as savage and barbaric. But it was thought at that time that the punishment has to be exemplary and participatory as well.' The leader paused, then continued with a sigh.

'The deserters were bound to two trees. The other boys were told to come in a line and each one was asked to give a blow to each of the boys with a sharp 'dao'. It was a messy, bloody affair but the aim was twofold. Everybody had to participate in meting out the death penalty for desertion, that was the first. The second was to see who among our boys were bold and disciplined and courageous enough to mete out the death penalty to the deserters.'

Ron felt restless as the leader spoke. *Why is he bringing this up now? This is neither the situation, nor the time to talk about desertion in such a way.* He intervened, 'We have to forget many things, even unlearn what we had learned though certain experiences. The main matter now is... we have only five people left besides you. Now the issue is whether, from now onward, we stick together. Those who want to go even now, leave like the deserters, just get up and say so, and I will make all arrangements. As for myself, I am not leaving just now. The moment our leader is fit, I will take him, if necessary, after winter. These who are with me speak up.'

Everybody stood up and indicated their support.

'So, we are sticking together, sir, all of us have voluntarily decided to stay with you.'

The leader could only mumble a muted thank you.

June was only too happy that the uncomfortable session had ended. She raised three cheers and everybody, including the leader, cheered lustily. It also greatly helped to dispel the gloom and the sense of dread and revulsion that came over them in the cave.

June felt she could breathe more easily

She saw that Ron was also slowly inhaling and then exhaling deeply.

'Will they come back?' June suddenly asked Ron. They were standing on the ledge. It had snowed lightly in the morning and the overcast sky held promise of more snow.

'Why should they? Today is the fourth day.'

'What if they do?'

'They won't. I sincerely hope they reach Assam safely. Our own safety also depends on that or on both of them getting killed on the way down. If they are captured, who knows, they may speak about the cave and then the enemy may come after us with full force. Our safety lies in either of them getting killed or them making it safely to Assam. I don't wish them dead. Let them go down safely.'

June remained silent. Last night she had seen them coming back in her dream. They had come, holding their rifles above their heads in a gesture of surrender. Someone had whispered in her dream, 'Let's shoot them down!' And she had screamed 'No, no!'. She had woken up at that point.

33

It had started to snow regularly, but it was not heavy.

Slowly the world was turning whiter, crisper and cleaner.

The cave was never very cheerful to start with, but after the desertion by Amlan and Pran, June found it unbearably gloomy. She blamed herself for not maintaining more friendly relations with the two. She felt an inexplicable rage towards Ron—a senior leader with so much of experience should have known, should have been able to anticipate that such a thing might happen!

How can I dispel this gloom which has set heavily on all our hearts? June thought anxiously. She realized that she would have to play a big role in boosting the morale in the cave. Ron was singularly incapable of reaching out to people, being always formal, stiff and proper. And the leader? He had become a very bitter man. He probably now knew that he was not going to make it alive to Assam. His behaviour had become irritable, distant, complaining. Even June found it very difficult to stay with him for a long time. He used to tell such good stories about his past experiences, it was a real pleasure to hear him talk. Now he had become a disgruntled old man, always bitterly complaining. Everybody in the cave dreaded their time of duty with him, which came to six hours each. June reduced it to two-hour stints by rotation and instructed everyone to talk cheerfully with him, to discuss light matters, crack jokes, talk about their own lives even when he had not asked them and to continue till he told them to stop or fell asleep. This soon had good results and the leader become less irascible.

The cold had really set in. There was no heavy snow but light powdery snow fell every day. She checked everyone's clothes one by one, and was appalled at their condition. There was one soft mink blanket which she immediately took and placed under the blankets of the leader who became very happy with that luxury.

Kumbang did a very practical thing. He took an old blanket, made a hole in it for the head and wore it over his padded jacket like a poncho. It made him look funny, but it caught on. Everyone did the same. It was quite effective in keeping them warm. Even Ron did it, joking that they were looking like a bunch of Mexicans from a cowboy movie. The leader liked it very much and awarded Kumbang a medal for innovation. The medal was nothing but the lid of the empty Vicks tin that he made Kumbang flatten and put a black twined thread through a hole on top. Ron solemnly pinned the 'medal' on Kumbang's jacket amidst clapping, after a short speech by the leader. Somehow everybody felt an affectionate respect for that ridiculous medal and June could feel that it had lightened the atmosphere and made everyone happy.

In the evening, while she cooked, she started singing loudly and others started to join in it. Ledo, the last foot soldier left in their group, started tapping out a beat on an empty plastic container.

The cave has become a real crazy house, but everybody, including the leader, seems to like it. At least I have been able to dispel the gloom that had started to set in, June thought jubilantly.

'We are living in a real crazy place, don't you think?' June asked Kumbang, 'I mean our cave.'

'We are ourselves crazy people to start with, otherwise we wouldn't have been here.'

They had come out to the ledge. Before them spread the plateau, covered with a blanket of snow. The sky, too, was a bright milky white and the mountains hazy.

'Let us go down,' June said to Kumbang. 'Let's go and see our old sentry post'.

The sentry post had been brought to the main entrance of the cave and made into a real pillbox with a stone roof.

'Are you sure you want to go?' Kumbang drew his poncho tightly around, indicating that it was very cold.

'A walk will warm us up. Come on, you lazy lout.' She started climbing down. Kumbang had no other option but to follow her down the ledge.

They walked over the ground covered with snow which crunched crisply under their boots. A cover of ice had formed.

They saw some animal droppings near the sentry post.

'Hey, look at that;' Kumbang said. 'They are most likely wolf droppings. They have turned hard and white.'

'Are you sure?'

'Has to be. We don't know of any other animal living around here. If there had been Himalayan bears, they would have gone into hibernation by now. We have never seen any bear pug marks, have we? Wolves, it has to be wolves.'

'I don't want to think about the wolves,' June said.

She went inside the sentry post, beckoning Kumbang to follow. They sat on the low bench and June started to hum a tune. She wanted to sing about the snow but she didn't know any song that had snow as a theme. Snow never falls anywhere in Assam so the songwriters didn't describe it. Only one famous short-story writer had written a beautifully imaginative short story about snow falling on the city of Guwahati. She told Kumbang about it, but he had not read the short story. 'How could you, you ignorant lout, it was probably written before you were born.'

June went on talking to Kumbang saying, 'Oh, oh' from time to time. Then she saw Kumbang looking at her intently. When he met her eyes he would look away, but again start staring at her when she was not looking. She could feel him staring at her breasts. She turned towards him and looked deep into his eyes. He smiled sheepishly.

'What's the matter, Kumbang?' she asked.

'Nothing.'

'There is something surely.'

'No, there isn't.'

'Don't lie, there surely is. You want to touch?'

'What?'

'You want to touch my breasts again, don't you?'

'Yes.'

'I know.'

He laughed, a low chortle of a laugh.

'It's very cold. I won't open my jacket. Warm your hand inside, but only for thirty seconds, okay?'

'Too short, but okay. Countdown starts from the actual touch.'

Through the side of the cape-like blanket, Kumbang gently pulled down the zipper of June's jacket, undid the button of her sweater and put his hand inside. He had to grope through the layers of clothing she wore until he touched flesh. He gently caressed her breasts and rotated his hand, trying to feel for an erect nipple.

'No,' said June softly.

Kumbang didn't listen to her. Slowly, he circled the nipples softly, one after the other.

June moaned and let out a long breath.

'Can I squeeze a little?'

'No,' she said tremulously.

Kumbang squeezed lightly, then a little harder.

After a few moments, June said, 'Time up.'

'Oh, just a little more.'

'No, time up.'

Kumbang took away his hand and breathed heavily, his fair face turning red.

'Now I will also touch you,' June said.

'What? You will do what?'

'I will also touch you.'

Kumbang was speechless.

June didn't wait. She put her hand over his crotch and caressed him.

'This time over the clothes,' she said.

She could feel his member, already turgid, coming to life and attaining hardness.

She tried to stroke its length through his clothes and squeezed the bulb at the tip. After doing it several times, she said, 'Thirty seconds over.'

'You can have thirty minutes.'

'You naughty boy!' June said and removed her hand. 'Next time, if there is a next time, I will feel it inside the clothes,' she said and laughed.

Kumbang stared at her with flushed face and shining eyes. Then he got up and went out of the bunker to a clump of tall bushes, away from her sight.

He is jerking off, June thought. A pleasurable warmth spread over her lower abdomen and inner thighs. She squeezed her legs and tried to fully enjoy the sensation that was coursing through her body with her eyes shut.

~

They returned with slow and heavy steps to the cave, walking silently and crunching the snow underfoot.

June hummed a popular tune. Kumbang pricked up his ears. It was one of his favourite songs. He immediately said, 'Please sing it loudly, please.'

After a pause, June sang, her voice floating over the snow-covered desolate sloping meadow. Kumbang started to hum with her…

'O take away all my wealth
All my belongings, and even
Snatch away my youth from me
But give me back my childhood.
The days of "Sawan" rains
The paper boat and the flowing waters…'

34

'PRADIP COMES FROM a broken family, you know.' The leader was talking to Ron. He had recovered from his ailment but had become very weak. His commanding voice, which practically remained unaltered during his actual illness, was now weak. It had lost its timbre. 'Take good care of him, Ron, he is a lonely and unhappy guy.'

June was also sitting nearby, unseen by the leader. She had always known Pradip as a practical, easy-going chap. She didn't want to hear any more sad stories. *I think I have enough pressure, enough worries already and I don't want to gather any more burdens.* She silently slipped off. Ron gestured to her to stay, but she ignored him. She went out of the cave. Kumbang and Pradip were under the ledge, preparing to come up. June gestured to them to wait. Then she climbed down the steps to the ground. The last foot soldier was manning the sentry post.

'Promise me, Ron, that you will look after Pradip,' the leader said.

Ron nodded, wondering why the leader was saying this. He had never observed any special relationship between them, any closeness! Aloud he said, 'If he requires any looking after, I will do it, sir.'

'He doesn't require looking after physically, Ron, it's his mind—he requires understanding and affection. He is quite young, should be about twenty-seven or twenty-eight, nearly as young as Kumbang. As I have told you, he comes from a bad family background. His father was an alcoholic who had squandered the family fortunes, selling off parcels of land when he required money. Then he brought in a young woman. After that, his two elder sons, who were much older than Pradip, drove him and the new woman out. Then the elder brothers divided the property, taking most of it for themselves and also drove away Pradip, his mother and a younger brother away from home. They now stay in a small house in a plot of land at the other end of the village which was given to Pradip and his brother.'

Ron went on listening.

'I have been to their house, and I have seen their abject poverty! Pradip couldn't even continue his studies. I brought him to the organization, had him trained, kept him under my eye and then without his knowledge went to his village again.'

'What did you do there the second time?'

'I called the elder brothers, put the fear of God in them and forced them to do an equitable distribution of property amongst the brothers, that too in writing, in the presence of village elders. Now Pradip has a sizeable share, so does his brother, and their mother doesn't have to work as a domestic help any longer. She can look after the home and her goats and ducks. They get enough paddy from the sharecroppers to last them the year and beyond.'

'Does Pradip know this?'

'I told him long afterwards.'

'Why did you do it, sir?'

'Well, I had taken Pradip away from his home.'

Ron remained silent, waiting for the leader to continue.

'I thought I owed him and his family this much. It was within my powers to do it in those days when our writ ran nearly everywhere. Don't you think it was the right thing to do? One less unhappy family?'

'You were certainly not wrong.'

'Good you think so! I know I have not done a wrong thing. As I said, one unhappy family less. How much good do you think a man can do in this world?'

'Why does he need special care, sir?'

'He has some sterling qualities.'

Ron waited for the leader to continue.

The leader paused for some time as if he was trying to overcome the tiredness that struck him from talking so long.

'Ron, remember always, loyalty is a stand-alone virtue. You have to nurture a sapling of loyalty wherever you find one. It is not a personal loyalty to me alone that Pradip has or for the organization—it is much deeper and ingrained. I will tell you how I realized that. Pradip once got orders to do a bombing run. You know the procedure. He got it by drawing lots. Then jobs were fixed and ten boys drew the lot. His job was to plant and detonate two bombs in a busy intersection near a police thana. On all three sides, there were big and small shops. In front of the police post was a busy restaurant and a big grocery shop. The first bomb was to go off in front of the restaurant and the second one in front of the thana a few moments later—so that the police would be rushing out to the road as expected after the first explosion. The main target was the police which had a very heavy force in the thana. And Pradip got orders to do this run.'

Ron immediately thought, *There must have been many civilian casualties in that plan.* He asked, 'Did everything go off according to the plan?'

'Pradip refused to carry it out.'

'Refused!? Did you say he refused?

'Yes.'

'Why?'

'Because his village was only two kilometres away and lots of people from his village went every day to that busy intersection. The youth from the village would regularly go there in the evening to loiter, talk, shop. They had nothing else to do anyway.'

'Did he have any issue about the civilian casualties that were likely to happen in that bombing run?'

'No, not as such. We all accept the fact that in our struggle there would be civilian casualties at certain times. It is unavoidable. That was not the issue.'

'Then?'

'He didn't want to do it himself because his fellow villagers were likely to be killed. Fellow villagers and even relatives, maybe cousins.'

'So he had no issue with killing people—he was only

concerned about casualties among people belonging to his village or his relations. Did he know the consequences of such a refusal?'

'How much he actually knew I don't know, but when he refused I told him what he would face if he refused. About a court-martial, even the death penalty as punishment for gross insubordination.'

'What did he do then?'

'He still refused.'

'Ah, so he had no compunction about killing people, but those he killed must not be his own fellow villagers or relatives. What do you make of that?'

'Well, Ron, that's what I'm trying to explain. It's a sense of deep loyalty to fellow kinspeople, be they fellow villagers, or relatives. That loyalty even under the gravest personal threat was what caught my eye. I thought, and I think I rightly thought so, that those who have the seeds of loyalty can have genuine loyalty to a struggle, to an organization, to an idea. I realized that it was a virtue that needs preserving. Don't you think so?'

Ron didn't answer the question straightway. He asked, 'What happened then?'

'I lost my temper at first, really blew my top. Then when I realized what I already told you, I cooled down a little and saved him. The tasks were set by me, those ten tasks including the bombing run. I postponed it on the pretext that it required more investigation. It was good that Pradip refused to do the job only before me. It would have been really difficult had he refused to do the run before others. He was, I thought, too valuable to lose.'

Ron had to agree with the leader's assessment.

The leader said, 'That's why, Ron, I have asked you to take care of him. His loyalty is ideological. You have to nurture it.'

'Yes, yes,' Ron concurred.

The leader was nearly panting from the exertion of talking for so long. He said at last, 'Ron, I thought I should tell you about this, because I think I am not going to make it.'

35

I DREAM OF a ruined palace!

A palace with colonnades—long rows of them.

Colonnades on both sides of a long passage stretching as far as the eye could see!

And I am moving through them—through the columns of ancient stone—through a world full of echoes seeped with sadness. My breath also causes echoes here, like the hissing of unseen serpents.

Yes, unseen serpents that have twisted themselves around the columns. Their hissing releases cold blasts of air like the breath of death. Yes, death also has breath like fire-breathing dragons.

I feel the breath touching my forehead, my neck.

But I am no longer afraid of death, not any more.

I have come into terms with it. I have developed a fond longing for it.

In the long colonnaded passage of whispering sadness, as you move along it, you see the faint outlines of an arched door full of light at the end. And there I see a white draped figure shimmering in the light. That is death! I have seen it—death.

When I try to talk about these feelings to Ron or June, they always try to change the topic. They don't want to talk about death. I try to tell them it could be beautiful, but they try to avoid the subject altogether. I don't blame them. Who would like to talk about death in this cave where the possibility of death stares you in the face every moment of the day.

But I am no longer afraid of death. I know it.

~

June had to sit through all the lyrical descriptions of death that the leader had lately started making. She could see that he was deteriorating fast. His muscles seemed to be slowly melting away. He tired easily but could still talk clearly. June, in fact, felt that his eyes had become brighter and his mind sharper.

The leader didn't want to stay inside the cave. He insisted that he be carried out of the cave to the ledge where the winter sun shone for quite some time. June could see that he looked at the scene before him with hungry longing. He eyes drank in everything—the swirling mists caressing the mountains, the pale blue sky, the snow-laden mountains tops. He had asked June to prop up his head with pillows so he could have a better view. It had become very cold—only when the winter sun shone and there was no strong cold wind did the ledge become comfortable. June would make the leader wear a monkey cap, tuck the mink blanket around him and cover him with a thick rug atop his stretcher bed before the boys carried him outside. Kumbang built a tent-like contraption which covered his head from the wind and snowflakes. The leader thanked Kumbang profusely and asked, 'Do you still have the medal I gave you?' Kumbang showed him the tin medal that he kept pinned to his jacket and the leader beamed with happiness.

At times he would ask everyone to leave, because he wanted to stay alone. And he would gaze at the distance in a vacant way as if he was deep in thought. Then he would doze off and sleep peacefully. When he got up from sleep, whoever was on duty near him would alert June and she would soon bring a small cup of black tea and two biscuits. He would enjoy the sips of tea with biscuits and then he would start talking. Invariably, he would start talking about death, which June dreaded.

When the leader slept again, June would look at the mountains and the landscape all around. Heavy winter snowfall had started already and the ground was covered with snow in most places. In the nooks of the creeks, snow had frozen to hard ice. The weather had become exceedingly cold and the valleys looked black and forbidding. Even the trees, laden with snow, looked like hunchbacked witches.

The sloping mountain faces were already covered with a mantle of snow but the straight steep faces showing the jagged stone surfaces took on a dirty ochre colour. *These mountains*, she thought, *are really abodes of sadness*. The sorrow of millions of people living below had risen as vapours to the sky had reached the mountains and frozen.

Fragments, snatches of thought fleetingly passed through her mind, and feelings too, but, nothing stayed for long. Everything was transient.

Her past life seemed so unreal now, not only the past but the present too.

Will this life have a new beginning, a new meaning one day? June asked herself longingly. *What does the future hold?* She had no clue, neither had she any hope, no straw she could try to grasp.

Long ago, when she was in the small hill town, she along with her cousins had visited a soothsayer. He was a wizened old man, with a sparse beard and burning eyes. He used to sit in an open room under a thatched roof. He was specially renowned for his predictions and his ability to cure madness and the disease of love. People came from long distances, bringing children with mental disabilities or hysterical young women to him. The hysterical women were tied to various trees near his dwelling and they would either rant, curse loudly or stare at the world with bright eyes full of hate. The relatives who brought the unfortunate women would silently cook their meals under the trees at a distance. The soothsayer talked very little and read fortunes only from the flowers he asked people to bring.

June remembered how startled she was when he said, 'I can't cure the madness that is within you. You had a hard life then an easy one. In future, you will have a very difficult life, then again an easy one. You will have a late marriage and a good husband like the god Siva.'

'But be aware,' he had said 'you must control the madness that is within you.'

He told her cousins similar things. 'Good things always come with a good husband!' said the older cousin, making fun of the old man's predictions on their way back, trying to interpret his words. But the old man had not spoken about any inner madness in the case of her cousins.

I must now be going through the phase of a very hard life, June thought. *Yes, it must be so, because I am no longer myself. These days I'm often confused about what is happening.*

Only the other day, right out of the blue, Ron suddenly told her, 'I have many things to tell you, June.'

She was surprised, but didn't show it. Ron continued, 'I don't know how to or whether I shall be able to say them all….'

Her instinct immediately told her what he might be thinking. She decided not to let him know that she had understood. She simply gave him a faint, sweet, enigmatic smile and looked away towards the mountains.

The late afternoon sunrays shone on the mountains, painting them with a light orange hue where snow had accumulated.

Ron waited for some time behind her, his feet making small nervous scuffling sounds. Then he went away.

And June felt as if she was left on the ledge holding an urn of emptiness.

She wanted to cry, but couldn't understand why she wanted to do so.

It is Kumbang, more than anybody else, who is really unsettling me, June thought. *He is turning out to be a real bore.* Kumbang had started calling her elder sister, 'baideu', at every opportunity he got. More so in front of others, Ron specially, even the leader.

That day she was sitting in the sun on the ledge. As usual, she felt disturbed. The leader was sleeping peacefully under the hood Kumbang had built. The sun was a little stronger that day and the pleasurable warmth seeped into her bones. She saw Pradip and Kumbang coming towards her but she waved them away. They would only make useless small talk. What more was left for them to talk about, except about their personal lives? In the last few days they had only talked about their lives. Even Ron had talked fondly about the naughty antics of his engineer brother and reverentially about his father, a teacher who only believed in Gandhian non-violence. June increasingly found such talk tedious and commonplace. And she didn't want to know any more details of her companions' personal lives because they avoided the subject that would have interested her—their love lives.

Kumbang returned after some time. This time he was alone. He went to the sleeping leader, looked at him for some time, then plopped down beside June. He started without any preamble.

'Have you noticed one thing, baideu? You must have.'

'What?' June replied reluctantly.

'Ron sir is in love with you.'

June remained silent

'Don't you know it?'

She wanted to answer him truthfully.

'It's not that I have not noticed his behaviour or the way he looks at me, if that's what you mean, Kumbang.'

He nodded.

'But I am not so sure. It is not that I have not received attention from men before so I do know a thing or two. But I am really not sure. And I want to tell you something.'

'What?'

'Do you think it is the time and place for such thoughts?

'Love doesn't require a particular time, place or environment to blossom. Does it? Do you really believe it does?'

'I don't know. I have never really thought about it till now.'

'If he says anything to you, declares his love,' Kumbang said gravely, 'if he says something, don't ignore him.'

June got angry. She looked at Kumbang and told him rather brusquely. 'I don't know really and I don't want to hear or think about it.'

'Why, June baideu?' Kumbang was not put off by her anger.

This time June was really flummoxed for an answer. She maintained a brooding silence.

'Is it because of something you have heard?' Kumbang asked in a soft voice.

'You will never leave me in peace, you pest, will you?'

Kumbang smiled but silently waited.

'I have heard he has someone who is waiting for him.'

'I have also heard the story,' Kumbang said. 'It may not be true, and…'

'And what, Kumbang?' June could guess what Kumbang was going to say. Her tone was challenging.

'After so many years,' Kumbang started, a little

hesitantly, while June held his stare unblinkingly. 'After so many years, the feelings may not be the same any more'.

'That is the problem, Kumbang. Over the years, the feelings, the emotions, disappear... evaporate.'

36

Two ravens flew through the leaden, glassy sky.

They flew silently, but Ron felt as if the vibrations from their strong wings were carried by the air down to where he stood—and engulfed him.

The pair of ravens circled above the trees and then perched on two tall branches. Then they started cawing—rasping, coarse irregular, random cawing. To Ron it appeared like an ill omen. What are these two doing here? Why haven't they flown off to warmer climes? Don't they migrate in winter to the terai forests below the mountains? No other birds could be seen because of the snow.

He had heard that ravens are harbingers of ill omen, but also remembered reading somewhere that some people consider the raven as a sacred bird too.

He remembered his own childhood, when quite a few ravens used to come along with the common crows to the place near the kitchen tube-well where the soiled dishes and utensils of the house were washed. He remembered that the helpers in their house used to shoo them away, throw pebbles and sticks at them. They didn't mind the noisy crows very much, but the ravens they considered as inauspicious. The ravens were quite fearless and didn't fly off as easily as the crows did but just jumped from one perch to another, always keeping a keen look-out with their red fearless eyes.

And he also recalled how he and his younger brother would sometimes bring out their homemade bows and the arrows balanced with duck feathers and try to stalk the ravens and the crows. Like great hunters they would stealthily approach the ravens and let their ineffective arrows fly. But most of the time, the hunters were spotted by the ravens who would let out one or two hoarse caws and with one or two flaps of their strong wings, fly off disdainfully.

It was totally unlike the behaviour of the cowardly crows who would create a real ruckus at the sight of the bows and would noisily fly in circles at a safe distance above.

Ron suddenly remembered his younger sister. She was a tiny tot then, who had just started going to school. She would cry when she saw them going after the crows and ravens with bows and arrows. She would come out with a little rice tucked into the hem of her frock and place it on the edge of the kitchen courtyard. Then from a distance she would watch, waiting for the first crow to jump down and peck at the three small heaps of rice. If the crow pecked at the first portion it indicated good news, the second the arrival of a guest on that day and the third, bad news.

It was always the first crow and the first peck that mattered because immediately after that, all the crows would come down and crowd around the rice, cawing loudly. The crows were supposed to give the message: 'Masters, cook well, guests are coming, cook well, and cook enough so that we also get leftovers …'

Ron smiled at the memories.

'You are smiling, sir? Pradip commented.

'I remembered something from my childhood.'

'Childhood memories are always very pleasant, if you had a childhood, that is.'

Ron was taken aback at Pradip's comment. He remembered the leader's words and said hurriedly, 'You can't be more right, Pradip.'

~

In the evening, June sat near the fire, the rough blanket encircling her legs on the grass pallet. With the cold increasing, the pallets were rearranged near the fire and all of them slept there, except June who had to sleep in her old alcove a little distance away. Otherwise, she would stay near the fire with her feet wrapped up.

A stone enclosure was built for the fire, which was tended day and night and a strong blaze was kept going.

The sky, the air, the surroundings were like glass, a glass wall of impervious cold. The sun, whitish and mild, shone in a clear sky. The morning mist rose like a bank of clouds rolling in, slowly enveloping everything in a shroud of sadness. On some days, there would be so thick a fog that Kumbang said it could be scooped out with a spoon. Ron took every precaution to see that no one would catch a cold. He made a rule that everybody had to bathe with warm water only, and of course, no one protested. They didn't have buckets, so they took whatever containers they could get—rusted tins, empty plastic jars—and filled them with hot water. They had to rush through the bath otherwise the water would turn cold.

At night, June dreamed about Joy. She felt he was calling out to her from somewhere, but she didn't see his image ever. The voice always floated in from somewhere and she often saw a sky lighted by halogen lamps like lights of a big city seen from a distance, the orange glow spreading in a swirl.

Hallucinations! I am having hallucinations, June thought with a shiver.

He was urgently calling her towards the lights. *Is he calling me to Delhi, where I have heard he is staying?* She felt a great turmoil and a pervasive restlessness.

She got up with a start.

The cave appeared to be in seamless darkness. The fire had gone down, but in the glow of the embers, Kumbang, who was on guard duty, was toying with some wooden pieces. She looked at him. His face was dark and he was looking ridiculously hunched in that poncho of his.

Is Joy also thinking about me? Is it telepathy? June asked herself. *Otherwise, why am I thinking about him? The last I heard of him was that he was in Delhi, doing some business and doing well. What shall I do if I get to Assam safely? What after that?*

She thought about Ron. *What is he going to do?*

She felt he would propose to her—or maybe not. She

was not sure. She didn't want him to say anything as she didn't know how to respond, what to say.

When they were discussing the situation in the valley, much of it was guesswork, but they knew that they would possibly have to lie low for a long, long time. They would have to find the lost threads and set up linkages. The whole process had to be re-thought anew.

Joy was incessantly calling out to her. She could feel it quite often. She would be able to find him if only she could leave the cave. Surely he must be trying to maintain contact with her through her cousins, now that he was rich. She still remembered her cousins' mobile numbers. The only thing she needed now was a mobile.

Maybe I can live with him for a year or two. I need a breather, a real breather. I am still living in the claustrophobic cave and experiencing hallucinations. A hallucinating madwoman, that's what I have become. Oh, what am I thinking? Useless thoughts, useless thoughts! There is still a long way to go—but I hope I can eventually get to Assam.

That day the leader was feeling better. His voice was stronger, his mood upbeat; he was talkative as well as introspective. They were all sitting around the fire, when he began talking, 'We all started with a dream, didn't we, Ron? What do you say? We all aspired to achieve a goal, an idealistic one.'

'Undoubtedly it's true, sir.'

'Started with a dream,' the leader spoke with meaningful emphasis. 'But we have entered into a nightmare, a never-ending nightmare.'

'Would you put it that way, sir?' Ron said.

The leader ignored him. 'Starting with a dream, we have entered a nightmare,' he repeated. 'Where have we gone wrong?'

June suddenly became all ears. Why had he raised this topic? There must be some reason. She felt as if the leader's last question hung in the air, becoming something palpable! The leader then directly asked Ron.

'Ron, what would you say? Honestly.'

'I don't know what to say,' Ron started in a cautious way. He could feel the eyes of all the other members on him. 'We knew very well, right at the beginning, that we had embarked on an uncertain path. We knew it wouldn't be easy.'

He paused for a moment, then continued, 'Nobody can foresee what you may find when taking such an unknown path.'

'That is very true,' the leader agreed, then said, 'but that is past, is it not?'

Everybody was startled by the leader's emphatic tone. June could feel their minds working, could guess their uncertainty.

They remained silent.

The leader continued, slowly, a little ponderously and with emphasis

'Hear my words. I will not live to see those days. I want to die early to free you all from the bondage I have imposed on you. Now, don't interrupt, nothing can change the reality of fate, of destiny. Hear me.'

They waited, not daring to look at each other.

They were afraid that he was going to utter unspeakable words, that he was about to commit the most serious blasphemy.

He said slowly. 'We do not know what is happening below in Assam. Everything must be in disarray. Our organization is likely to be in shambles. And those who are outside the country may choose to live in the old way.'

He paused and looked at the expressionless faces of the five people before him one after the other, and then continued, 'I have thought long and hard. Probably the time has come when we have to work openly within the democratic set-up of the country, without losing our ideals. It will be tough, very tough. It will be more difficult than the armed struggle we had started, but my feeling is that it is required as a strategy, not mere tactics. It possibly cannot be avoided. We now have to find out how to do this. That is the task.'

Everybody remained silent.

'What would you say? Does anyone have any ideas?' the leader asked them, addressing them collectively.

Nobody replied

'Do you think that what I am saying is a kind of betrayal?' His tone was challenging. 'I don't think so. It is not. I have nothing to betray now. The situation is no longer as straightforward as it appeared in the past. As time changes, circumstances change, people change. I don't want you to reply to my questions unless you think about them deeply and honestly. Long training makes it hard to do certain things. But remember and think over my words—working within the democratic framework is required as a strategy, not as mere political tactics.'

Three days later, after three days of silence with no discussion at all about what the leader had said, he died at night, peacefully, in his sleep.

37

THE SOUND OF small silver bells tinkling unseen amidst the rolling mist—that was a memory June would carry for a long time.

Looking down at the winding mountain road, they could see three people coming slowly towards them. At first their figures appeared and disappeared through the thick mist of the morning. The mist looked like multilayered veils, luminous in the morning sunrays.

The figures became more distinct as they came nearer.

Three persons with two small donkeys laden with clothes, provisions and a small wooden box were walking. One was a Buddhist lama in a reddish robe with a blanket thrown over his shoulders, rolling prayer beads in his hand and mumbling a mantra. He was an old man and his companions were even older than the lama, but were lay helpers. While one of them led the two donkeys, the other carried in his left hand a small silver bell, which he rang in his own rhythm and with his right waved a yak-tail fan over the wooden box from time to time.

The box must contain a holy talisman, thought June.

She immediately told herself it was an auspicious omen, a sign of deliverance.

She bowed her head chanting the only Buddhist prayer she knew '*Om mani padme hom*!'

~~~

They had buried the leader with full military honours.

They had discussed whether they should bury or cremate him. Ron said, 'All our people have been buried, not cremated.' With suppressed sobs, June told them that the leader had spoken of burial and indicated a spot too. June remembered how she had sharply chided the leader when he had spoken those words. She also remembered his laughter, open and free-flowing at her anger.

Everyone waited for her to show them the spot.

'It is near that central outcropping of stones in the meadow.'

They had buried him there silently, ending the solemn function with a gun salute.

The next morning, after a heavy meal cooked on the cave hearth for the last time, they had left the cave, one after the other. June knew that everybody had mixed feelings, but did not express them. No one spoke, and except for Ron, not one of them even looked back.

They crossed the mountains at a rapid pace.

It was strange moving without the stretcher of the leader. Tears welled up in June's eyes and she let them flow freely, not caring if the group saw her crying.

Their clothes were tattered and frayed, making them look like ragamuffins. Ultimately, it was Kumbang who found a way out. He wore his jacket inside out. The inner lining of checked multicoloured cloth looked quite funny on him but served the purpose. Others followed suit.

On the third day, they crossed the snowline and came to the heavily wooded forest below. On the fifth day, they reached the hill top from where the hanging bridge could be seen.

They stopped there. Before them was a deep gorge and the hanging bridge spanning it—a bridge between them and tomorrow. Beyond that was a world populated by humans with all their vices, a new set of dangers, pitfalls and possibilities.

From the top of the hill, they stared at the bridge till the late afternoon mountain dusk, along with the cold and mist, rolled in through the deep canyon and engulfed the bridge and its surroundings in its smoky embrace.

From the hill top, they went to the mountain path below, the one that lead to the hanging bridge, which they would cross at the crack of the dawn on the next day. When they reached it, they didn't step into the path but kept to the bushes and trees at the side. Pradip and the foot soldier remained in the front, Kumbang and June in the middle and the rear was brought up by Ron. They had great difficulty secreting their weapons in the folds of their garments. They couldn't wear the practical ponchos devised by Kumbang for fear of attracting attention. At the most, they could drape the blankets around their shoulders, and that was what they did.

They waited in the bush by the roadside patiently. From where they were, the hanging bridge couldn't be seen as it was around a bend in the mountain road. *Why are we waiting on the edge of the road like this*, June thought, *silently waiting like birds of prey, as if we are expecting danger?*

The narrow deep gorge between the two mountains suddenly widened after the bridge like the mouth of a funnel into a deep, multilayered valley covered by large forests, which appeared dark blue through the mist. It was as if two long arms of mountain ranges were encircling and embracing the valley below. Sunlight had fallen in patches on the valley which was covered by a patchy blanket of clouds.

There must be villages there, June thought, but it was not possible to go down to the valley from that place because of the steep drop of the mountain face. The only way down was after crossing the bridge.

From the top of the hill, from where the bridge could be seen, she had looked at it in sheer fascination and also a sense of dread. The bridge appeared to be floating in the swirling mists of the deep canyon. *Will we be able to cross it?* June thought worriedly and shivered involuntarily. The bridge looked rusty and discoloured, appearing and disappearing in the clouds of misty vapour.

Three stout cables were suspended between the mountain faces over which wooden planks were fixed. There were two more stout cables above from where wire suspenders went down to hold the lower cables. Side rails completed the whole picture. The planks were placed with gaps in between so that when there was heavy snowfall, the snow wouldn't accumulate and weigh the bridge down. Buffeting winds also passed through the gaps.

It was then that they heard the tinkling sound of the silver bells!

Fog was still quite dense on the road when the lama, his two companions and the donkeys appeared.

June suddenly saw Kumbang making a move. He gestured to her to follow him.

Before June's surprised eyes, Kumbang rushed into the road and bowed low before the lama and then as the party reached closer, knelt before him with folded hands. June could iguess what he was doing and why. She also followed suit and knelt before the group a little behind Kumbang as the local customs dictated. The lama appeared to be pleased. He beamed and intoned something which seemed like a blessing. The two companions also appeared to be pleased at the couple showing respect to the lama and making a small offering to the box atop the donkeys. They grunted their approval and the man who was ringing the bell let loose a long pealing.

June couldn't but admire Kumbang for taking out the few soiled notes of the local currency and making an offering to the box. *The sly fox*, thought June admiringly, *with his hillman-like features he so easily blends with the group*. The lama resumed his rosary ritual and the journey along with his two helpers and the donkeys. June and Kumbang easily merged with them and went along with the little donkey procession.

They went towards the bridge. Kumbang could talk in the local language, which he had picked up during his trips to the villages near the camp. He had a natural talent for picking up languages. He learnt from the lama's companions that they were on their way to the main monastery in the east for the winter. June also could understand the language though she couldn't speak it fluently like Kumbang. She remembered a very small Buddhist temple in the far village beyond the camp where she had been on one of her trips to that village. It was as far as they were allowed to go from the camp. It was over the snowline, a small stone and wooden hut where there was an altar with a statue of the Buddha in it. A couple of lamas stayed there and the village people used to pray there. In winter, the monastery would close down and the lamas would leave for the main monastery to return only in spring. Half the population of the village would also migrate.

She was grateful that the lama and his entourage didn't think the sudden appearance of two bedraggled figures from nowhere was strange but warmly accepted them as travel companions.

When they approached the bridge, June could see that the sandbagged gun encampment and sentry posts on the side of the bridge were empty. There was nobody in the guard house on the other end either.

They then crossed the bridge.

As soon as they reached the flat-roofed guard house surrounded by the low stone wall, two men suddenly came out from the back of the house. June was relieved to see that they had no weapons. They came to the lama, knelt before him and invited the whole party into the guard house compound. The lama accepted their invitation and entered the guard house ushered in by the two fawning guards. The two companions, after tethering the donkeys, also followed suit.

Kumbang gestured to June to stay close to the wall of the building. June suddenly saw through the corner of her eye that Pradip and the other boy were swiftly crossing the bridge and rapidly getting into the woods beyond.

Where is Ron? June looked around frantically. *He is nowhere to be seen. Hasn't he seen us crossing? Where has he gone?* Then she suddenly glimpsed Ron's back disappearing into the thick bushes beyond, making her wonder when he had crossed the bridge.

They were across the bridge at last! The relief was so overpowering, so palpable, that it brought tears to her eyes. Then she saw Kumbang urgently gesticulating to her to follow him. She went and both of them silently walked past the guard house, crossed the mountain road which was a little wider at that point, and then silently melted into the forest beyond.

The sound of tinkling silver bells remained with June. She felt as if she was hearing then constantly within her head, the rapid cadence followed by a slow rhythm.

When the group reassembled after crossing the bridge in a dense patch of forest, the fog had lifted and the afternoon air was crystal clear. They formed a tight group and held each other in a tight embrace. Their unspoken words, the fervent embrace and the sound of their deep breathing revealed their feelings. Only June cried unabashedly.

A light, pleasantly cold breeze was blowing from the mountains and it created a murmuring rustle in the leaves of the trees above. All of them were completely drained by the long trek in the morning, coming down from the mountain, crossing the bridge and reassembling. Kumbang and June plopped down on the ground and immediately went to sleep in the fragrant earth under the trees covered with dry leaves.

Ron smiled at the scene before him. He asked Pradip and Ledo to mount guard on two sides for a three-hour shift and sat down on the ground near a tree.

Survival—that will be the first priority once we go back to Assam, Ron mused. *Much as I would have liked our group to stay together, I know that it will not be possible. We don't know what is happening in Assam. In such times, to keep all five of us holed up in one place would be suicidal. I shall have to find out some way to keep my four companions safe.*

A bird called out and the trilling voice immediately caught Ron's attention. It sounded so familiar. He tried to recollect the name of the bird. What was it? Yes, it was the laughing thrush. Ron felt very happy to be able to identify the bird. He leaned against the trunk of the tree above him and with his eyes shut, kept on listening to the birdsong. Soon he fell asleep.

~

They climbed mountains, each progressively lower than the previous one, on their constant trek southward.

They decided to avoid all human habitations, though the temptation for human company and a hot meal was quite strong. Habitations and fields became much more frequent as they went south.

June observed that, on the last leg of the journey, Ron was unusually silent and seemed to be very deep in thought. Others also sensed it and could only guess what he might have been thinking.

On the third night, which all of them knew would be their last night in the hills, after they had set up camp for the night and eaten together before retiring, Ron suddenly cleared his throat loudly. Immediately, everybody became alert. It was a clear signal that he was about to say something serious.

They waited in the darkness for Ron to speak.

'Do you acknowledge me as your commander, your leader, and are you willing to follow my orders?' He paused. The question hung heavily in the air. He then put it to them one by one, calling out their names. Everybody replied in the affirmative. And from the tone of their voices, Ron could make out that they were not lying.

'Good, I am grateful,' Ron said in a grave level voice 'then follow my orders without any question.'

He heard murmurs of assent.

'Tomorrow we enter Assam,' an emotional urgency entered his voice. 'We don't know what we would find there. At this point our greatest duty is to preserve ourselves to live to see another day. For this I am making two teams, the first with Pradip and Ledo and the second with June and Kumbang. You shall travel separately and directly move out of the state. Decide where you will go. You shall memorize a few email addresses through which we shall make contact. You have the money I have given you equally out of what we could bring out. Go, and remain safe for another day.'

Everybody was silent.

'Kumbang,' Ron said, 'you can go to Goa. I will also come and join you two there, ha, ha—that's if I can make it.'

Emotions swirled through June. This time it didn't bring tears to her eyes but a lingering sense of emptiness, of a dry sadness tinged with solitude.

~

They rounded the shoulder of the last hill. It was a low hill covered with tall trees.

There were trampled paths all around with droppings at places—it was obviously an area frequented by herds of wild elephants.

June gasped when she saw the open valley of Assam sparkling in the misty sunshine of mid-morning. She leaned against a tall tree on the top of the hill. A wide shallow river meandered amidst wide expanses of shining white sandbanks and rounded stones, pebbles and flowering bulrushes. The morning breeze rustled the surface of the river, reflecting the sunlight from its surface.

'Pradip, you start first,' Ron gave out his last command. 'After half an hour Kumbang and June will follow.' Pradip drew himself to his full height, stood at attention, saluted and left with his companion, without even looking back once.

After half an hour it was June and Kumbang's turn.

They also saluted. Ron, his face impassive yet kind, stood there like a lonely sentinel.

June could restrain herself no longer.

She ran to him, embraced him and buried her face in his chest to stifle her sobs. She heard Ron saying to Kumbang, addressing him by his first name, 'Jayant, take care of June.'

She left, with Kumbang following her.

Once down the hill, she stopped and looked back up. There he was, his figure small under the giant trees, standing still like a statue, bronze and immobile.

She felt the mountain breeze on her cheek, the air carrying a fresh fragrance of the forest, and heard the trilling of the thrush.

She turned and then rapidly went downhill with Kumbang towards the shallow river. After crossing it, she would reach Assam.

www.ingramcontent.com/pod-product-compliance
Lightning Source LLC
Chambersburg PA
CBHW050339030726
47503CB00008B/2521